"**What gives you the right to turn up where you were never invited? All because I dared to walk out on you?**"

Darcie rose on tiptoe to slam her truth right into his face. "There was never going to be a good time to leave you. There is always some imperative deal you're working on, you're always pushing for more." Part of her admired him for that. She'd learned from him.

Defeat swelled within her. Overwhelming, horrific defeat that brought forth bitter blame as the implications sank in. Her application to care for Lily would have to be delayed. Lily who was so little, so lost, so lonely—Lily who mattered more than anything.

"You can't think about anyone beyond *yourself*," she berated Elias. "It is always about everything *you* want and need and it always has to be right now. Well, I have wants and needs too, and I needed to get married. *Today*."

"If that's the case, then let me fix the problem I've created." He seethed wildly. "You *need* to get married today? Then fine. You can marry *me*."

USA TODAY bestselling author **Natalie Anderson** writes emotional contemporary romance full of sparkling banter, sizzling heat and uplifting endings—perfect for readers who love to escape with empowered heroines and arrogant alphas who are too sexy for their own good. When she's not writing, you'll find Natalie wrangling her four children, three cats, two goldfish and one dog...and snuggled in a heap on the sofa with her husband at the end of the day. Follow her at natalie-anderson.com.

Books by Natalie Anderson

Harlequin Presents

The Greek's One-Night Heir
Secrets Made in Paradise
The Night the King Claimed Her

Billion-Dollar Christmas Confessions

Carrying Her Boss's Christmas Baby

Once Upon a Temptation

Shy Queen in the Royal Spotlight

Rebels, Brothers, Billionaires

Stranded for One Scandalous Week
Nine Months to Claim Her

Jet-Set Billionaires

Revealing Her Nine-Month Secret

The Christmas Princess Swap

The Queen's Impossible Boss

Visit the Author Profile page
at Harlequin.com for more titles.

Natalie Anderson

—

THE BOSS'S STOLEN BRIDE

HARLEQUIN
PRESENTS

HARLEQUIN®
PRESENTS™

ISBN-13: 978-1-335-58420-5

The Boss's Stolen Bride

Copyright © 2023 by Natalie Anderson

Recycling programs
for this product may
not exist in your area.

For questions and comments about the quality of this book, please contact us at CustomerService@Harlequin.com.

Harlequin Enterprises ULC
22 Adelaide St. West, 41st Floor
Toronto, Ontario M5H 4E3, Canada
www.Harlequin.com

Printed in U.S.A.

THE BOSS'S STOLEN
BRIDE

For Soraya—again and always! I'll always be grateful for your whip cracking and cheer!

CHAPTER ONE

ELIAS GREYSON HADN'T just mastered the art of avoiding inconvenient emotion, he'd perfected it—effortlessly ignoring not just his own, but that of all others. To be unmoved in the presence of histrionics made all decisions—be they business or personal related—clinical and easy. Rage, recriminations, pleas or guilt trips didn't penetrate his armour. No matter the provocation, Elias Greyson didn't overreact, didn't get riled, and definitely didn't make snap decisions in the heat of the moment because he always ensured any heat was eliminated from important negotiations. Emotional reactions led to poor outcomes, he found. A measured, rational, controlled response was right. And if he were occasionally accused of being a cold-blooded, ruthless bastard, so be it.

But today Elias was having a rare, *imperfect* day. Irritation burned up his spine—an irritation that had been building for the last two weeks. He checked the clock on his computer and said irritation roiled higher. He gritted his teeth. Of all the days for his ultra-efficient assistant to finally fail him. He was flying from London to the US in a few hours and he wanted everything organised ahead of take-off. His latest acquisition target, a venture capital firm based in San Francisco, was proving a difficult fish to hook. While the company would be useful for Elias to push further into the North American market, its chief exec, Vince Williams, considered 'values' to be important. The old man's diligence searches went beyond company balance sheets all the way to any prospective raiding CEO's silk ones. Apparently perfect Vince had been married to his childhood sweetheart Cora for over fifty years and was known to disapprove of a party lifestyle. Elias wasn't quite the playboy he'd been a couple of years ago but apparently the fact he was still single was enough to cause 'concern'. It was ridiculous and Elias would be informing Vince of the fact face-to-face at their meeting tomorrow.

He would also be taking over the firm regardless. But he'd prefer the acquisition not to be hostile, which is why he'd wanted everything squared away in an impeccably prepared offer that would be impossible to refuse regardless of anyone's 'values'. So the last thing he needed was to be let down by his primary assistant a few hours before departure.

Darcie Milne had never been late. Not once in the two and a half years she'd worked for him. Usually she was seated at the desk just outside his office before he even arrived, and he arrived early. But that chair was still empty. He snatched up his mobile. The text messages he'd already sent her remained unanswered so now he actually phoned her. It went straight to voicemail.

'I need you in the office. *Now.*' He stabbed the screen to end the call.

Five more minutes crawled by. His supposedly superior ability to ignore inconvenient emotion slipped as a sliver of worry crept in and splintered his concentration. Had something happened to her? Every muscle tensed. Where the *hell* was she?

At that exact moment his office door was flung open. Darcie Milne stalked in and slammed the door behind her.

Elias stared, rooted to his seat, jaw hanging. Because Darcie Milne was not wearing her customary office attire of loose-fitting white shirt, even looser grey trousers and boring brown brogues. In the dreary uniform's place was a knee-length cream-coloured skirt and matching jacket. Both of which were a little too large on her frame, but that skirt offered a very rare glimpse of her ankles and calves and creamy skin. The room temperature shot up at least ten degrees.

He forced himself to shut his mouth and lift

his gaze, but she wasn't looking at him anyway; her focus was on his wide wooden desk between them. She'd not looked him square in the eyes once in the last fortnight. *That* had irritated him, too. He'd gone for so long without being bothered by her. Frankly he'd been proud of the degree to which he'd remained impassive to her presence. Until two weeks ago, that is. Because two weeks ago she'd—

'What the hell time do you call this?' he growled, refusing to think of that night. But the effort cost him his customary cool.

'You don't remember anything outside of the current deal, do you?'

Shocked by the uncharacteristic bite in her tone, that unfamiliar irritation almost overwhelmed him. Darcie had never given him moody attitude. She—like he—was usually calm. She was diligent. Dutiful. Sure, she sometimes challenged him but only when required, only ever about business and always very coolly. She was quite often correct, too. Not that she was some docile doormat, more an efficient, aloof automaton. One he refused to look at for too long. Only today—now—he stared at her. *Hard.*

'What's going on?' he clipped.

She put a file on the desk before him. He

could see the familiar neon sticky tags she preferred and the neat notes in her clear print.

'I've narrowed it down to five. That ought
not to be too taxing for you to have to interview,' she said.

'Interview?'

'The applicants for your executive assistant.'

'*You're* my executive assistant.'

She stiffened and her expression was different again. 'Have you really forgotten the resignation letter I emailed you a fortnight ago? I
left a paper copy on your desk, but I know you
read the email. I got the receipt.'

Oh, he'd not forgotten. He just knew his
rights. He glared at her grimly. 'Your contract
requires *three* weeks' notice. As you sent your
letter only a fortnight ago, there's one week left.'

'But as I have so much accrued annual leave
owing I'm taking the last week of my notice
period as a holiday. You're paying the remain-
der of my accrued holidays out.' She shrugged.
'It's a lot.'

Something rippled beneath his skin at the un-
ashamed defiance—sass—in her reply. She'd
never crossed that line. Not until that night in
Edinburgh.

'So you're going on holiday now?' he asked.
Where was she going in that ill-fitting cream
suit—a nunnery?

'Correct.'

Elias had lost many employees in the past and initially he'd been determined not to give a damn about Darcie's unexpected decision to depart. Then he'd decided to get her to change her mind. But he'd not addressed it with her directly yet. Truthfully it had taken more assimilating than he'd expected, especially after that other issue.

But while he refused to beg, he couldn't stop himself from testing her loyalty. 'You realise it's a terrible time.'

'It's *always* a terrible time,' she said, her voice clipped. 'There is always some massive deal on the table that you need everyone all over. It wouldn't matter when I handed in my notice. It was always going to be an inconvenience to you.'

'It's far more than an inconvenience.' The admission growled out.

'You're being dramatic,' she said crisply. 'You'll be fine. You always are.'

His jaw dropped. Dramatic? 'Not fine.' He scrambled to keep on track. 'You know this deal is—'

'Imperative? Vital? Does the company's future hang in the balance because this is the biggest deal you've ever done?' She cocked her head and actually rolled her eyes at him. 'They always are, Elias. But admit it, this one is all but sealed. The meeting tomorrow is a mere formality. You don't need me there. You don't need anyone. Besides, I bet you've already lined up the next deal and doubtless it's even bigger than this one. Am I right?'

He stared at her. Who was this woman? Where had calm, capable Darcie gone?

Her mouth twisted. 'I knew it. There's no *final* deal for you. You're always on the hunt for the next passion project before you've finished with the one right on the table in front of you.'

His skin tightened. Passion project? Was she talking business mergers or personal ones? Elias made no apology for his voracious appetite. At least he was honest about it. Which was more than she was. There was passion and hunger within Darcie, too. He'd known that from the moment he'd met her. He'd just been pretending not to remember ever since.

'I'll double your salary.' Somehow the offer slipped out.

But it didn't have the desired effect.

Storm clouds swept into her eyes, enhancing the blue, and he couldn't have moved if he'd tried. Because then Darcie put both palms down on his desk and leaned across it to vent. 'I have given you almost every hour of every day for nearly three years. I've never before denied you. But enough is *enough*.'

He blinked, shocked by her sudden vitriol. Darcie was never emotional at work. Not even when she'd worked thirty-one hours straight and was paler than tracing paper with smudges beneath her eyes. Not even then had she lost her cool with him. She was always professional. Or she had been. Until that one very strange, very unforgettable night. Then she'd been anything but.

'It's *just* like you to have forgotten.' Lightning fury flashed from her. 'Do you know I don't have to be in this office at all today? I'm only here because of misplaced loyalty.' She dragged in a breath and twisted the knife. 'To my colleagues.'

'*Misplaced* loyalty?' The comment had him in a car racing towards a cliff edge. To the ravine he'd avoided at all costs. Until now. Because now he was pissed off, and the emotion was all-consuming. 'To your *colleagues*, Darcie? Not to me?'

'No.' She lifted her chin. But she still didn't quite meet his gaze. '*Not* you.'

'But—'

'I can't stay to argue, Elias,' she snapped. 'I don't actually have time.'

Why not? But he couldn't seem to ask. He

couldn't seem to think. He could only stare at her as now she finally stared right back at him and her captivating eyes were full of things he couldn't stand to see—resentment, anger, *hurt*.

'Don't you even want to know why?' she breathed.

His obliging executive assistant, always anticipating, a step ahead of everyone except him, had turned on him. The quietly efficient woman who didn't fawn but who got everything done was gone. In her place, radiant with energy, was a beautiful, furious firestorm.

'Today is my *wedding* day and yet I've *still* come running at your damned summons. But this is it. I'm done.'

Wedding? The shock ripped through him like a tornado, turning up—

Her *wedding* day?

Before his heart could beat she stormed out, slamming the door behind her and leaving Elias struck still in the suddenly cavernous room. Bile burned his mouth as his body launched its own violent response. He brutally swallowed it back, but bitter rage gripped him regardless as her words reverberated.

Wedding day.

He hadn't been spoken to like that—hadn't been excoriated by someone's scorn—in so very long. Who the hell was she marrying? She didn't have time to date anyone. And how *dare* she after—?

He vaulted out of his seat and strode to the door, flinging it open to glare across the office. Naturally Darcie was nowhere to be seen. She must have sprinted. Was she that desperate to escape him or was her speed to get to her groom? His fury mounted.

Without exception his remaining staff had their gazes glued to screens; apparently all were suspended in eerie still silence. Of course, Darcie was the one who'd usually stare back him and ask what he wanted. Or she had been. Until these last two weeks.

Can you please pretend this never happened...?

To say nothing. To do nothing wasn't Elias's usual style. He didn't know why he'd said yes to the *second* of her breathy requests that night. But he'd been saying nothing and doing nothing regarding Darcie Milne for months. He was practiced. Besides which, it had been the right thing to do.

'*Where* did she say she was going?' he demanded, too furious to bother pretending they hadn't heard every word of that argument. 'Is it *really* her wedding day?'

One of the assistants attempted a smile. 'It's so romantic, don't you think?'

No, he did not. It was *not* romantic. It was a sham.

'What do you know about it?' He turned towards the woman. And how come he didn't? Because he spent more time with Darcie than anyone.

'Not much.' The woman swallowed, her smile fading. 'It only came out at her farewell party last night.'

A party that he'd known nothing about and certainly hadn't been invited to. Insult to injury, much? A rosy cloud of rage misted in front of him. Never mind that he never socialised with his staff. Had Darcie sipped champagne the way she had a fortnight ago? When she never, ever drank. In all the nights she'd travelled alongside him, not once had he seen her touch alcohol. Until then.

Come upstairs with me?

Had she invited some other guy to her room the way she'd invited him?

'Where's the wedding?' he rasped.

'The register office in the city.' A wary response.

She was getting married in a register office on a weekday morning? Something was off. Darcie was off—just now she'd most definitely not been herself. This wasn't—couldn't be— real. It certainly wasn't right. He nodded, his feet moving fast. Because as far as Elias Greyson was concerned, Darcie Milne wasn't getting married anywhere today.

Not to anyone.

CHAPTER TWO

DARCIE PACED THE CORRIDOR, keeping her gaze on the main entrance. It was only ten minutes until the allotted time for the ceremony, but all she could see was Elias's expression as she'd fled his office fifteen minutes ago. He'd gone white—piqued because she'd snapped and not jumped to his summons. There was nothing more to his annoyance. No deeper emotion. There was never any real emotion with him. He was just too used to getting his own way. And right now she needed to forget the long-standing infatuation that had led to her making a colossal fool of herself a fortnight ago. She sucked in a breath and slammed the door on that mortifying memory once more.

It. Was. Over.

She wouldn't see Elias Greyson ever again. She was about to marry someone else. As long as her groom actually arrived.

Her whole body suddenly ached like she'd come down with insta-flu. She checked the time again and her nerves exploded. Why *wasn't* Shaun here already? She knew he'd been reluctant but she'd thought she'd convinced him. Darcie would do anything for her best friend and Shaun had loved Zara, too. And Lily was the one—the *only*—part of Zara that lived on. That little girl needed them. There was no way Darcie was letting Lily remain in the foster system any longer than necessary.

Shaun had eventually agreed when Darcie assured him she had enough money saved to give him what he needed to build his business. She'd have agreed to anything to secure Lily's future. And she'd have just enough left over to stop work for a little while.

In a few months Lily would start school and Darcie could return to work while also helping Shaun. Now that she had the experience of working for Elias Greyson on her résumé, she'd get any number of jobs through an agency. Unless Elias didn't give her a good reference. Which, given she'd just yelled at him, was a possibility. Nobody raised their voice at Elias and he certainly never raised his. But it would be too unfair if he held that one lapse this morning over her. For more than two years she'd worked all hours for him and yes, she'd been paid well. But for that last moment this morning she'd always remained in control of herself. Never once biting back the way she'd sometimes wanted. Never once saying anything inappropriate. Because she'd needed the job and he was her boss.

Okay, aside from today there was just that

one time she'd said something she shouldn't. But he'd agreed to forget it.

But she still couldn't forget his face just now. He'd truly expected her in the office today. He'd not even noticed that she and most of the others had gone for pizza last night for her to say goodbye. Of course she'd not included Elias on the email invite, knowing he wouldn't come, but it shocked her that he hadn't even known about it when ordinarily nothing in the office passed him by. He'd looked stunned. Part of her would've laughed if her stupid heart hadn't been breaking. Because her stupid heart had been his from the first moment she'd clapped eyes on his ridiculously handsome form. She had to work so hard not to look at him too much in these last two years...

But he'd not even cared about her resignation. Only that she hadn't been at her desk first thing this morning to see through this latest deal. Too hurt to admit, she stared at the floor and willed Shaun to arrive.

'Darcie? Sorry I'm late.'

She looked up, startled her wish had come true. Shaun hurried over, dressed in faded jeans and tee. She swallowed and forced a smile. It wasn't as if she'd gone to all that much effort either. She didn't even have a posy of flowers. But her treacherous mind reverted to Elias.

What would he wear to his wedding? Doubtless it would be a glamorous affair. He'd stun in a bespoke tuxedo and he'd have literally a model bride…

'It's okay,' she reassured Shaun as cold sweat slicked her back. 'Thanks. It's almost time.'

Shaun shoved his hands in his pockets. 'Haven't you sent the money over yet?'

'I haven't had a chance. I got called in to—'

'If I don't pay that deposit I'll lose the deal. You know I need it now, Darcie.'

She refocused and studied Shaun more closely. Sweat beaded on his upper lip and he fidgeted, moving from foot to foot as if he didn't want to remain in place.

'Come on, you know we're going to need this,' Shaun added impatiently. 'Transfer it now and I'll forward it right away.'

Darcie's inner alarm inside sounded.

You can't ever trust anyone.

She'd known Shaun for years. She knew his weaknesses. But she also knew he was fighting them just as she was hers including the doubt—that alarm—she was feeling right now. The assumption that she would be let down yet again by someone she'd thought she could trust was an automatic reflex she constantly had to combat.

'Can't it wait an hour?' she asked.

'I promised him the money yesterday, you *know* that.'

Shaun's frustration was increasingly obvious. The last thing she wanted was him walking out. This marriage would secure Lily's future and she *had* to trust Shaun to follow through. He'd been through the same system so he knew how important this was. But neither of them looked like they were about to marry. Neither exactly happy and blushing.

'Okay.' She nodded. 'I'll do it now.'

At least the task would stop her from dwelling on Elias. She leaned against the wall and pulled up her banking app, telling herself it was going to be okay. Yes, Shaun had faced hard times and, yes, he'd made mistakes, but he was pushing to do his best. And they'd be leaving here as husband and wife. What was hers was his and vice versa. She'd be doing the accounts for his new business and thanks to her time working for Elias, she actually understood all that stuff. It only took a few taps to transfer the money.

'All done.' She nodded at Shaun. 'It should be there now.'

'Great.' He pulled out his phone and walked farther along the corridor from her. 'I'll let him know the money's on its way.'

'We only have a few minutes,' Darcie called after him.

He nodded distractedly and turned away, already holding the phone to his ear.

'Darcie?'

Her heart stopped. Was she hearing things?

'Darcie!'

She turned towards the entrance. Elias Greyson was all imposing height and anger, striding in her direction in the manner of some vengeful warlord from medieval times who was coming to…to…grab her wrist?

Darcie was so shocked she froze. Never, in the almost three years she'd known him, had they touched. Not even to shake hands at her initial employment interview. And now he had her wrist firmly in his hand and it didn't seem as if he was about to let go.

'What the hell is this about a wedding?' he whispered furiously as he lifted her arm and inspected her fingers. 'No engagement ring,' he added accusingly. 'You've *never* worn one. Not ever.' His blue eyes sparked at her.

Her heart pounded. He'd noticed that?

'Not everyone is hung up on accumulating material possessions,' she muttered, horribly breathless.

'He's too cheap?'

Her jaw dropped.

'You cannot be serious.' His grip tightened

and sparks shot up Darcie's arm. 'You're really getting married?'

'Yes.'

'Here?' He shot a cursory, dismissive glance at the faded paintwork in the stale institutional building.

Darcie took the chance to glance down the corridor at Shaun. He was still on his call but had turned and was watching them with wide eyes. As she looked back she saw other people in the waiting room were staring at them, too. But then everyone stared at Elias. He was taller than most, impeccably dressed in that crisply tailored suit that cost more than most people's monthly wages, and had that air about him that commanded attention—efficiency, capability, authority. Naturally he didn't notice they were watching, and if he had he wouldn't care. He was so used to it he was apparently immune to any kind of self-consciousness.

'Yes.' She drew a breath.

'Wearing that?' He looked incensed.

She flinched at the horribly judgemental tone. Elias had never once commented on what she wore and the first time he did it was slung as an insult? She glared right into his beautiful, arrogant eyes, too angry to hold anything back. 'What does it matter to you what I'm wearing? Why are you even here?'

'Why do you think?'

'Because I'm taking my last week as leave?'
She furiously goaded him. 'Didn't you like that?
Was it a surprise? Can you really not cope with
my not dancing to your tune for *one* day?'

'It has *nothing* to do with that.'

Suddenly he was too close—towering over
her and still holding her wrist and near enough
for her to feel not just his heat or his strength but
his fury. Elias didn't get furious. Elias, as far as
Darcie knew, didn't feel anything particularly
strongly. Other than the unquenchable desire to
build his business. But now she was unaware of
anyone or anything else other than the intense
link suddenly forming between them—not the
feel of his fingers on her skin, but the searing
pulse of raw emotion. It was as if the veneer of
civilisation she'd cemented her soul in for so
long had been shredded and the danger buried
in there was exposed. The danger she'd almost
successfully avoided for so long—bar that one
lapse. But now, with his touch, with his taunt,
her control was torn.

'What I'm doing today is really *none* of your
business,' she whispered.

'Not my business?' he challenged silkily.

She froze as she saw a strange glint in his
eye. Her heart kicked. 'Elias—'

Another electrical pulse shot from his hand to her wrist, charging her blood.

'Who are you?' Shaun roughly interrupted them.

Elias's hold on Darcie's wrist tightened. 'You can't marry him.' His intense gaze didn't waver from her. 'You're not in love with him.'

Her heart stopped.

'I *know* you're not in love with him.'

She was so shocked, so horrified, she couldn't respond.

'I know,' Elias repeated softly. 'Because—'

'*Don't…*' Mortified, she finally whispered.

His jaw clamped and he glared at her, waiting for her to say more.

But she shook her head. He couldn't be here. Not now. Not putting everything at risk. It was too precarious as it was. 'Don't say it. Don't you *dare.*'

A white ring formed about his tightly held mouth while furious energy leapt in his eyes.

'Of course she's not in love with me,' Shaun said testily. 'And I'm not in love with her.'

A muscle in Elias's jaw ticked. Darcie wanted the earth to crater and consume her.

'You're the groom?' His question was so softly asked it was seemingly emotionless.

But Darcie knew different. Because *Elias* was different. Her spine prickled in warning because she knew Shaun would hear condescension and arrogance. Elias was the epitome of everything Shaun despised. Successful, wealthy, powerful, privileged. Like the man who'd got Zara pregnant with Lily five years ago. She turned and saw the expression in Shaun's eyes. Worse than sneering distaste, it was resentful defeat. 'Shaun—'

'This is nothing but drama, Darcie.' He shook his head. 'Maybe you're better off dealing with it with your rich jerk here.'

'Shaun!'

But as he backed away she didn't move. She couldn't, because there was still that hard grip on her arm holding her in place. And in less than two breaths, Shaun was gone.

'Darcie Milne and Shaun Casey?' a clerk called.

Darcie remained silent as she struggled to process the fact that her groom had just abandoned her. She'd known, hadn't she, that Shaun had been unsure. It was why she'd delayed making that payment until he was here, and if they hadn't been interrupted they would be getting married now.

'Darcie Milne and Shaun Casey,' the clerk repeated. 'Darcie and Shaun?'

She turned and stared up at Elias with savage bitterness. 'Now look at what you've done.'

'Better now than after the vows.' His tone was impassive but there was more than watchfulness in his eyes. There was wildness—a stormy emotion that she read as satisfaction and it destroyed her. Every last shred of self-control was obliterated in a tsunami of anger.

'How dare you,' she breathed. 'You swan in here, swaggering around as if you somehow know it all. That you have the right to assume and to judge and to change everything?'

'It's just a wedding,' he retorted. 'It's not like it's a matter of life and death.'

'And that's where you're wrong,' she flung at him. 'I *needed* to get married today.'

'Well, your groom is pretty weak if he fled just because I showed up.' Elias snapped back. 'He wasn't in love with you,' he added obstinately. 'He even said so to your face.'

'Of course he wasn't in love with me.' She nodded, bitterly, awkwardly hurt. 'Who would want me, right?'

A frown flashed in Elias's eyes, but she was too far gone to give a damn.

'Marriages aren't always some ideal romantic fantasy, Elias,' she said harshly. 'Sometimes marriage is a practical solution to a real problem. But you don't have any clue about real problems in your high-flying, billionaire party world.'

Elias stiffened. 'What's the problem?'

As if she was going to tell *him*?

He leaned closer, his fingers tightening. 'What's the problem, Darcie?'

She glared back, angrily marvelling at the arrogance and ignorance of him. He was literally blocking her path to where she wanted to go.

'I hate you,' she muttered. 'This is all your fault.'

She was furious with him for appearing—unannounced, uninvited, ruining everything she'd worked so hard for, for so long. His timing could not have been worse. And she was even more furious because part of her had leapt to life at the sight of him. The stupid hormone-driven sexual part that she'd almost managed to completely ignore. And it was firing up again.

'What gives you the right to turn up where you were never invited? All because I dared to walk out on you?' She rose on tiptoe to slam her truth right into his face. 'There was never going to be a good time to leave you. There is always some imperative deal you're working on—you're always pushing for more.' Part of her admired him for that. She'd learned from him. 'But you know what, Elias? This was *my* deal. My *one* deal. It was the only one I've *ever* wanted and it was my only shot to get it and you've *wrecked* it.' Her breathing quickened and her heart was racing and racing and she was terrified of bursting into tears.

'He's a jerk,' Elias shot back savagely. 'It was obviously never going to last.'

'That wasn't the point!' Darcie completely lost control, her voice rising. 'That didn't matter! It would have lasted long *enough*!'

Defeat swelled within her. Overwhelming, horrific defeat that brought forth bitter blame as the implications sank in. Her application to care for Lily would have to be delayed. Lily who was so little, so lost, so lonely—Lily, who mattered more than anything. As for the *money* she'd just transferred to Shaun—would she get that back from him? Or would he disappear for months like he had before? And she wreaked all that anger, all that futility, on Elias. The literal roadblock in her way.

'You can't think about anyone beyond *yourself*,' she berated him. 'It is always about everything you want and need and it always has to be right now. Well, I have wants and needs, too, and I needed to get married. *Today*.'

'If that's the case then let me fix the problem I've created.' He seethed wildly. 'You *need* to get married today? Then fine. You can marry me.'

CHAPTER THREE

For one crazy moment Darcie actually believed him and her raw reaction was extreme. Excitement soared so high her senses spun out. She heard nothing but her heart beating a refrain—*Marry. Elias. Greyson.*

Impossible hope filled her lungs so swiftly, so completely, she shot past the point of pain. But when she was finally forced to release it, cold reality hit and she laughed—a bitter burst that sprang from the deepest despair. 'Don't be *ridiculous.*'

His expression was rigid but his pupils had blown. 'I'm not.'

But Darcie didn't believe him. He was being snide and she was so *hurt*. She looked down and saw his big hand still wrapped firmly around her wrist. The sizzle of skin on skin would surely leave a mark. But as if it were possible to be branded by his one touch? She shook her head. She was so *pathetic*. He didn't want her. She knew that already.

'It wasn't a joke,' he insisted curtly. 'It just needs some organisation.'

His blithely unrealistic understatement re-

fuelled the remnants of her anger. He was beyond arrogant.

'As if it's that easy?' She'd worked for *months*
to get to this position and he'd decimated it in
seconds. 'We're not in Las Vegas, Elias.' She
sarcastically informed him of the banalities that
made his supposedly simple solution impossible. 'We're in England. There are forms that
have to be filed days ahead of time.'

'Isn't there somewhere north...' He frowned,
then his eyebrows lifted. 'Gretna Green?'

'Gretna Green?' This time her brief laugh
was more of a squawk. 'What do you this is,
some Regency romance in which we elope because I'm underage?' She shook her head. 'It's
the twenty-first century and even there we *still*
have to file paperwork weeks in advance.'

'Speed really is of the essence?'

Darcie couldn't wait any longer because *Lily*
couldn't wait. Lily, who was about to be shunted
into yet another foster home that would never be
good enough and Darcie would lose her last opportunity to provide for her. Darcie, who'd been
so single-minded, so determined that she'd put
up with every one of Elias's endless and outrageous demands. The guy was an inexhaustible
tyrant—ruthless and relentless in his requirements—and she'd borne it all in biddable si-

lence because she'd needed to, but now futility swamped her. 'It was. Yes.'

'And it really doesn't matter who the groom is?' he asked, puzzled and searching.

But Darcie saw no need to explain anything to him. Elias Greyson was unlikely to ever marry anyone and most certainly not her. When she'd first begun working for him, she'd soon learned he was a playboy who dated an endless array of socialites and models and influencers—all of whom tended to be slender or beautiful or well-connected or successful or more commonly, *all* of the above. Darcie wasn't *any* of those things. Definitely not slender, nor beautiful enough to wear slinky dresses, and she definitely didn't come from the right side of the tracks. She didn't dance at the right clubs, in fact long ago she'd danced at the absolute opposite of the right clubs, not that she could ever tell him that. She didn't have an elite education or spring from some society family. And unsurprisingly Elias had paid no attention to her as anything other than his dutiful assistant. She wasn't and would never be his type nor an appropriate match. And she knew that fact *intimately*. As all her anger flooded back she finally twisted her hand and jerked her wrist free of his hold.

'Just forget it and *leave*, Elias. You've done enough damage already.'

She turned her back on him. But just as suddenly her energy slumped. Her legs felt empty. So did her soul. Depleted, she was left bereft of everything.

Elias stared as Darcie literally sank into the nearest chair. This wasn't the flounce of a pouting creature denied her own way, it was the collapse of someone whose whole world had just shattered. Paler than he'd ever seen her, she gazed unseeingly at the floor and the trembling of her limbs was visible even from five feet away. His formerly impeccably calm assistant was in pieces and apparently it was all his fault. She'd never spoken to him the way she had. No one had spoken to him that way in *years*.

He winced. His limbs didn't feel all that steady either as he struggled to recover from her elated expression the split second after he'd said he'd marry her. But a breath later she'd broken and laughed in his face. That bitter, blameful laugh had then excoriated him, decimating his own surge of excitement. Now shame slithered through his cells, sweating out through his skin. He'd never screwed up like this. He'd vowed never to interfere with another person's personal life—never to be so arrogant, so controlling, the way his father was. The realisation that he'd just done exactly that was unbearable.

But honesty mattered, too. Intentions mattered. And Darcie intending to marry someone else... He'd thought she was a liar and that had infuriated him because betrayal did. He'd not been able to stop himself from chasing her here to find out what and who and now *why* was it so imperative she get married at all. Why so quickly? Was this some kind of residency issue? A work visa? But Darcie was English so that didn't make sense. *None* of this made sense. The only thing that was completely obvious was her distress and inwardly he still rebelled at the accusation that it was *his* fault.

I'm not in love with her.

That slimy coward had walked out on her the second he'd had the slimmest of opportunities.

Sometimes marriage is a practical solution to a real problem.

Elias glanced about and saw another couple glaring at him disapprovingly. Yeah, apparently he *was* the villain here, which was outrageous. Hadn't he just saved her from marrying a fool who clearly didn't want to be there? He looked back at Darcie. The despair in her posture made his discomfort snowball. He didn't have the desire nor the ability to deal with emotional problems. Ever. His parents hadn't exactly given him the skills with their toxic, unbalanced mess of a marriage. It was why he kept so firmly, so calmly, to business. But this was Darcie and she was alone and it was unbearable to watch.

He moved to hunch beside her chair. 'Where are your witnesses?'

She kept staring at the floor. 'We were just going to use the city administrators.'

'You don't have any family here?' he pressed. Why was that? Why hide this from those closest to her? Shouldn't a wedding be a big celebration? It made him more suspicious. 'Not even any friends?'

She didn't answer. He'd worked alongside Darcie for a long time and he'd never seen her like this. Was she really in love with that jerk even though she'd denied it?

No.

Every instinct rejected the idea and for more than one reason. She'd been more focused on venting her anger at him rather than running after the guy who'd just jilted her. Her devastation wasn't the guy, but the wedding itself. Whatever the reason was, he knew her marrying was imperative. He recalled again that momentary leap in her blue eyes, that unguarded response when he'd said he'd do it...and something hot churned in his gut. But then she'd not believed him. Her dismissal stung. *No one* dismissed him.

His steely resolve returned. Elias Greyson

did not fail. He did not allow it. And he hadn't built his business from the ground up without accumulating some organisational skills. Furthermore he could delegate. Just not to Darcie. Not this time.

'Come on,' he ordered briskly. 'We need to leave.'

Darcie didn't move. She couldn't.

'You need to get married, right?' Elias pressed.

She was too heartbroken to bother trying to explain to him about Lily. Elias Greyson was a playboy with zero intention of settling down and having a family. He would never understand.

'You have your go bag with you?'

At that she looked up into his eyes. 'No,' she said scornfully. 'I resigned, remember?

'We'll swing by and pick it up from your place on the way to the airport.' He ignored her sarcasm and went straight for solution.

Her place? The airport? What?

'You're wasting time. Let's go.' He literally hauled her out of the chair and wrapped his arm around her waist.

Being pressed this close to Elias was overpowering. She was tall but he was taller and so much stronger, and frankly she wasn't sure if she was walking or if he were half carrying her. Feeling the lean strength of him made her all the more weak and just as she realised how mortifying that was they got outside and his car was right there and Olly his driver was studiously not staring at her.

'You know Darcie's home address, right?' Elias checked.

'Of course.'

Darcie folded herself into the farthest corner of the back seat and stared at her phone. Shaun hadn't messaged her. She sent him a quick text asking if he was okay. She didn't dwell on the money she'd transferred only ten minutes ago. There was no point. Her plans were ruined. Elias said nothing; he was busy tapping some thesis on his phone. Back to the deal, no doubt.

When Olly pulled over she immediately opened the door.

'Thanks for dropping me home,' she muttered stiffly. 'You don't need to come in.'

'No?' Too bad. Elias wasn't letting her walk in there alone. He got out of the car and matched her steps. With every one his disapproval grew. Why did she live in such a run-down, unsafe area? That Olly had never told him where she lived made him inexplicably angry. He'd have done something about it. He stood beside her, clamping his jaw to stop his annoyance unleashing as he followed her up the stairs and watched her unlock the door. He moved inside before she could stop him. And then he stared and all the anger that he'd thought he'd got back under his control emerged again.

'Do I not pay you enough, Darcie?' he asked softly.

It wasn't even a flat. It was a sparse and uncomfortable bedsit with a narrow bed, no sofa, no oven, just two hobs that didn't look like they'd been used recently. Her clothing hung neatly on a wooden stand. The grey trousers and white blouses that were so familiar to him and somehow made him even more annoyed.

'What do you wear to relax?' he muttered beneath his breath.

Of course the room was so small that she heard. She shot him a look. Right. She *didn't* relax. She worked all the hours for him. She was always willing to accept an extra project. He didn't even ask anymore; he just handed them to her because he knew she'd get it done. And he'd paid her more than enough, of course. But this was such a small place in a hellish part of town so what was she doing with the pay cheque? Was there debt? Yet he couldn't see how she'd accrued any because she'd not got tertiary qualifications until she'd started working for him. So then what? Why?

Far too late he realised he didn't know anywhere near enough about her. And he didn't like it. So that was going to change.

He caught sight of her travel bag tucked under the small fold-up table and grabbed it.

'What are you doing?' Darcie asked.

'What you want,' he replied coolly, hefting the bag in his hand and opening the door for her. 'We're getting married in Vegas, Darcie. And we're going there now.'

CHAPTER FOUR

DARCIE DIDN'T KNOW WHERE—or how—to start. They'd been on this plane for half a day already and Elias hadn't asked her again if she was serious or why she needed to get married. He'd simply acted on her demand and remained silent ever since. She'd been angry and shocked but now she was too scared to say anything in case he changed his mind. In case she woke up—because this had to be a dream, right? Because every so often she glanced across the aisle and caught him watching her and he had the oddest expression in his eyes. Ordinarily Elias was cool and focused and seemingly devoid of emotion. But right now? It looked strangely like *amusement*. But that just couldn't be right.

As usual they sat on opposite sides of his luxurious private jet, diagonally facing each other in the roomy reclining chairs. His legs were stretched out and apparently he was reading, as was his custom, but she was aware he hadn't turned the page in nearly twenty minutes.

She stared at the cover of the book. She'd found one like it on one of the first flights she'd taken in his private jet and had thought it belonged to the pilot. But it had been Elias's reading material for the flight. Not a report, or business journal, but science fiction. The guy read stories of survival in extreme, hostile, other planetary environments. Escaping from this world right here. She didn't understand why he had to. Because Elias's world was perfect, wasn't it?

He had a level of excellence everyone around him was expected to meet and he didn't ever let emotions get in the way. He didn't respond to emotional outbursts, either. Unmoved and impervious, he didn't flare with anger but simply turned away as if he had some inner force field repelling emotional manipulation. If an employee disappointed, they were dismissed. Initially from the room. Ultimately—if the disappointments were repeated—from the firm. There was no volatility or raging; he just had barriers. Though she'd never thought he was cold, nor careless, just *controlled*. He didn't have the time for hysterics or anger. Or even— she sometimes thought—enjoyment. The only outward satisfaction she'd ever seen upon the successful signing of a deal was little more than a nod. He'd put a tab on a bar for his employees to splurge, occasionally he bothered to show, but if he did he'd barely have one drink and then leave. His mind was always already on the next deal.

Or the date no doubt waiting for him.

Yeah, there were the women. Or there had been. But they never lasted and there'd not been many in recent months. Okay, any. And yes, she was tragic for knowing that.

But what he was, was a workaholic. She really didn't understand why because surely he was wealthy enough. Yet no one worked harder than he did. Not even her. And every one of his employees was stupid keen to impress him. Herself included. She didn't know why it mattered so much, only that it did. And it was daft because she deeply knew how impossible it was to please people. It didn't matter what else you did, you only had to make one mistake and it was all over. And today Darcie Milne had made a massive mistake. One she had to address. Soon. Absently she rubbed her wrist. She still felt the warmth and weight of his hand on her skin.

She shivered at the memory and muttered her thoughts before thinking better of it. 'Are we really going to Las Vegas?'

'I was flying to the States anyway,' he drawled. 'This is simply a sidebar on that journey.'

She stiffened at his uncharacteristically sardonic tone. 'So glad it's not an inconvenience.'

Elias actually chuckled.

Darcie had to grit her teeth to stop her jaw

falling open. This really was *amusing* to him? When was Elias *ever* amused by anything she said? As she stared at him, she saw challenge build in his eyes. He was waiting for her to say something more.

But she didn't. She couldn't. Because *this* time she thought first. She remembered what was most important. Lily. She had to focus on Lily. Because if there was the slightest chance Elias would follow through on his mad proposal, she had to take it.

Elias sprawled back in his seat, disappointed that Darcie hadn't said anything more and wondering what on earth had happened to get her to this level of desperate. Anyone else and he'd be confident about getting to the bottom of whatever the problem was in minutes—and equally certain it wouldn't be anything requiring a remedy as drastic as marriage. He could find other solutions to all kind of problems without breaking a sweat. But this was Darcie and he knew her attention to detail. If Darcie felt it was imperative to get married, then it was imperative. So *why* did she need to be wed so swiftly? When was a marriage ever a 'life and death' situation? His imagination ran riot. Was there some stalker she was hiding from? Was it a shotgun wedding—was she *pregnant*? He almost growled. Not to that guy, she wasn't, so if she was pregnant, then to who?

Come upstairs with me?

Something in his veins simmered at the echo of a hesitantly whispered question. Was *that* why she'd flirted with him so abominably the other week? Was she desperate to find a father for her unplanned pregnancy? He had to count to ten before he could breathe again. Now his curiosity wasn't just eating him up—his conjecture was growing wilder by the second.

But as much as he wanted to, he refused to ask her right now. She'd never spoken to him like that before. But before, she was his employee. Now he was no longer her boss and he couldn't order her about. He would wait until she was ready to speak to him. He wanted her to *want* to speak to him. And right now she clearly didn't.

During a flight like this Darcie would usually work through her checklist, making sure all the deal preparations were in place while Elias read because he was usually ready. But he wasn't ready today. He was astonished to realise that not only had he not thought about the Williams deal in hours, he had zero concentration to give it now and even more shockingly didn't give a damn. Because his curiosity ran unabated. He flicked through his files on his phone, accessing the résumé the temp agency had originally sent when they'd put Darcie forward for a position at his firm. But it didn't tell him anything he didn't already know. He wanted to *understand* Darcie, and it was a shock to realise he knew nothing of actual substance about her. Nothing personal.

Fancy cheese. Yeah, that was about it. He knew she liked fancy cheese. Because at one event early on in her employment he'd watched from a distance as she'd surreptitiously sneaked a piece of soft brie from the buffet table at the back of the room. Her reaction had been both gorgeous and gauche. He'd kept watching, wryly amused as she'd tried so hard—and failed—to resist sneaking another. Then another. And then he remembered that working late one night a few weeks later he'd noticed her growing pallor and it dawned on him—belatedly—that she'd not eaten. He'd been on an adrenaline rush and forgotten about food, plus he was supposed to have a late dinner date. But Darcie had had nothing. He'd gone to the office fridge and found some cheese and watched the colour return to her cheeks. Her deep inhalation, her sigh of contentment, her appetite *satisfied*…he'd got inexplicably angry.

'Why didn't you tell me you hadn't eaten?' he'd challenged her. 'Why didn't you complain?'

She'd offered the faintest of smiles. 'It's not in my job description to complain.'

'It's your job to ensure *all* details are met. You can't do that if you're not properly fuelled.'

'Well, if we're considering blame, then perhaps it's your job—as my employer—to factor in proper breaks for your workforce. It's late and we've been going nonstop for hours.'

It was one of the rare times she'd challenged him—with a hint of insolence that had barely surfaced since.

That night Elias had planned to celebrate prepping the deal with his date of the day. But he'd cancelled. He'd never stopped to truly consider why before. But he'd got sidetracked watching Darcie Milne eat cheese. And from then, he now acknowledged, he'd ensured such snacks were always available in the office. Over time he'd discovered it wasn't just cheese she was partial to but dried fruit—apricots, mango, apple—and nuts—walnuts, cashews, macadamias. She was like a little mouse who needed frequent feeding because she point-blank refused to attend business dinners with him. If they were abroad she retreated to her hotel room to work. He'd not argued with her decision. In fact he'd appreciated the barrier it kept between them. They were professional, never personal. But he'd always ensured there was a platter available for her. But she'd touched none of the supply he insisted was kept on the plane today. He pointedly gestured to the plate the flight crew had put on the table.

'You're not hungry?' he prompted her.

She shook her head.

He didn't like her silence. He didn't like the bruised look returning to her eyes. And he certainly didn't like the hot feeling tightening his gut.

His rule was to reject responsibility for how someone else *felt*. He always, always maintained emotional distance. After the hellish years with his father's coercion and his mother's misery, he'd rejected such a future for himself. Yet he hadn't been able to stop himself not just reacting to Darcie now, but provoking her in turn. And his reaction wasn't only irritation any more.

At the register office she'd been so compelling he'd been unable to release his hold on her. But she'd barely spoken since lambasting him then. He knew she was striving to regain her self-control and it was taking quite some doing—just like the day he'd met her. He'd never forgotten the emotion she'd tried and failed to hide during the interview. Fear had widened her eyes. He'd almost dismissed her as too nervy to cope with the relentless hours he frequently required in the office. But that same thing had made him take a chance on her. She'd not only wanted work, he'd sensed she'd desperately *needed* it.

Frankly he hadn't been afraid to use that need—hungry workers were driven and focused. Turned out none more so than Darcie Milne. She'd not allowed any distractions to interfere with her performance. She'd been available almost any and every time he'd asked. The one exception she'd stipulated was a two-hour stretch on Sunday afternoons. She'd made it clear nothing could interfere with that and given how accommodating she was the rest of the time, he'd respected it. Though he'd long wondered what the appointment she kept so religiously was. Even when they'd been abroad she'd locked herself in the hotel room for those two hours for a phone or video call. But he'd never asked.

He'd known from the first that she was smart, that she could grow into someone indispensable. And she had. Two weeks from when the agency had sent her he'd offered her a permanent position at four times her agency rate. Then when he'd found out she was working towards some qualifications online late in the evening when she wasn't working for him, he'd insisted on paying the tuition fees. He was reaping the reward of her diligence anyway. But even with that extra workload, she'd never broken down, never lost it with him for asking too much—not even after they'd pulled all-nighters to get deals ready. It was a miracle in his experience. Prior to Darcie he'd burned through executive assistants. He wasn't volatile but he knew his expectations and demands on their skill and time were extreme. For those who could hack it, it was great. Those who couldn't left. Many had left. And because of his father's infidelity with his secretary Elias never mixed business with pleasure. The moment he'd offered Darcie Milne a job was the moment he filed her in the *do not touch* category.

Do not think about her beyond the professional. *Do not* wonder about what she did at night when she wasn't working, and certainly *do not* dwell on who she may or may not do that stuff with. Yet shockingly Darcie Milne sometimes slid into his dreams. He couldn't control those. So for a time he'd been determined to prove she wasn't his type. He'd dated other women the absolute opposite to her. He'd refused to get hung up on one individual he barely knew and who was utterly out of bounds. Only his dating had become more sporadic in these past few months. It was because he'd dived even deeper into work.

But he'd battled an inappropriate arousal from the second she'd stormed into his office this morning. That mood had been brewing these last two weeks and now it exploded. *Want*. Such bone-aching, endless want. Painful and intense, it was building into an unfettered firestorm of craving that was almost, *almost* uncontrollable.

Sex was a physical release. But the emotion and expectation of relationships—the burden of someone else's feelings beyond immediate gratification—he'd mastered the art of avoiding those. He didn't allow strong feelings of his own. Lust was recreational and love didn't exist. He liked his life straightforward, and his inter-actions with women were *very* straightforward. He always made it clear he wasn't looking for a wife. Some were fine with that while some had pretended to accept it, but thought they might change his mind. They never had. Never would. As for children? No. People screwed up their kids. But he wasn't going to because he wasn't having any.

But Darcie was different to him. She had more emotional intelligence. One time she'd shot him a shockingly disapproving look when an analyst had turned in sub-par research and Elias had let him know. He'd caught her sooth-ing the guy after, which was irritating because it wasn't as if Elias had yelled at the guy. He never yelled at anyone. He'd never allow himself to lose that level of control. She'd told him he could be very 'dismissive', which had irked him more than it should. But the fact was her people skills made the office run more smoothly and he didn't want to lose her. She was a key asset in much of his success, and Elias liked success. He liked the challenge of taking on a competitor and beating them. He enjoyed researching—coolly, rationally assessing the qualities of each investment or acquisition. He picked winners. He was good at it.

He spread his fingers, still feeling her warm, fragile wrist, as he considered what she'd said she needed now. To be married. Darcie *herself*, he realised, was a prospective acquisition for him personally. If he were to list the attributes of an ideal partner, she would fit most. Calm—usually. Not demanding—usually. She had a similar work ethic plus she already understood his needs and not only accepted them, she worked well alongside him. At least in the business sense. She could give him the 'values' he was lacking. She would, he decided, make a *perfect* wife. She wouldn't ask too much of him emotionally. And the fact that they had undeniably shocking chemistry was quite the juicy cherry on top.

'Are we landing already?' She suddenly sat up.

'Yeah.' He stretched the tension from his

spine. 'And we're all booked in at a chapel. We'll go there right away.'

Her eyes widened but her chin lifted and he felt that anticipation ripple through him again. Was he actually enjoying himself? He'd not done something this rash in, well, ever. This was spontaneous, quite possibly insane, and while it would be easy as anything to stop, he really didn't want to. He wanted to see just how far Darcie Milne would go with this.

Her luscious lips parted, but she said nothing as she stared at him.

'Isn't that what you wanted?' he asked blandly.

That spark flared in her eyes. The one he'd not seen enough from her—*challenge*.

At the sight of it he almost purred inside. Yeah, to his amazement he was enjoying himself. Immensely.

'Because whatever it is you want, Darcie,' he added, 'I'm here to deliver it for you.'

CHAPTER FIVE

DARCIE STILL WASN'T sure her voice was going to work and certainly wasn't sure of what she was going to say. They'd quickly cleared customs and the waiting chauffeur had driven them straight to a chapel in an outrageously large limousine that had given her plenty of space from the man formerly known as her boss. Now she hovered just inside the doorway while he conversed in smooth undertones with a gloriously neon-clad receptionist.

Sick with nerves, she checked her phone again but there was still no message from Shaun. Taking a breath, she put it in her pocket and finally let herself look at Elias properly. She'd struggled not to stare at him for the entire flight. Correction, she'd struggled not to stare at him for *years*. Tall, dark, devastatingly gorgeous with his lean, muscular frame and hair that needed rumpling and shoulders that deserved to be clung on to…the guy was a long, lush glass of impossible.

'It's a veritable mix-and-match platter,' he said with a sardonic lift of his eyebrows on his return. 'We can choose any number of things, including variants of our vows depending how flowery you want to get.'

She couldn't appreciate his looks now. This was all too real and impending panic made her stomach churn. 'Elias—'

'Would you like to freshen up after the flight?' He grasped her arm and steered her along the corridor and into a private room. 'This is our dressing room. I'd assumed I'd wear a suit but perhaps you'd prefer me in denim?'

'Elias.'

He was on a rampage of sarcasm-edged activity—determined to prove that he could arrange this. Even when it was ridiculous. But he wasn't going to stop until she told him to. Until she told him *why*. 'I can't let you do this.'

'Let me do this?' It was a coolly spoken challenge, but his hot gaze tilted her world on its axis all over again. Elias didn't talk to anyone like this. He didn't act like this. Ever. Swift yes, but not rash. Not impulsively.

She swallowed. 'Try to help me.'

His focus narrowed. 'You said you had to get married. Today.'

'Yes,' she agreed. 'But the reasons are complicated and they're really not your problem.'

'Are they not?' he queried silkily. 'I thought this was all my fault. I thought I'm the ogre who ruined everything.'

'You are,' she ground out, trying to rein in her flaring temper all over again. She dragged in a calming breath but with him being so in her space it was hard to think. The combination of shattering disappointment and frustration and futility meant she was losing her already slim grip on herself. 'But while I appreciate all your effort to try to fix things...' She shook her head and mumbled. 'I should have said all this hours ago.'

'Why didn't you?'

'I got *so* mad...' She closed her eyes. She'd got so *hurt*. So frustrated—she'd wanted to make him feel something, to expose *any* kind of emotion. She'd wanted to lash out and make him pay for stunning her with that hit of hope and of sheer *want*. But like she could tell him *that*? She'd not been able to tell him what she really thought for years but as for admitting such mortifying and unrequited emotion?

'Did you want to see how far I'd go, Darcie?' he asked softly as he stepped towards her.

She didn't know how to answer that. He lightly put his hands on her waist. So lightly. But she stilled, completely.

'Testing me is a little dangerous, isn't it?' he asked.

'No. Because I don't think you're dangerous.'

Only he was. Dangerous for her heart. Right now it was skipping every third beat.

'No?'

They'd never stood this close. Any time they'd inadvertently brushed too closely—getting into a lift or passing in a narrow corridor—one or other of them had always quickly moved off. But not today. Today his grip on her tightened and she didn't step back like she should.

'I'm sorry,' she mumbled, dropping her gaze, desperate to hide the swarm of emotions his touch was unleashing. That mad desire to provoke him resurged. What was with her inner rebel coming to the fore?

'No. You don't get to say sorry and expect me to just forget about it.' His voice was husky. 'You don't get to walk away without a real explanation. Not this time.'

She didn't mistake the softness of his voice. 'Elias...'

'Why don't you just tell me what the problem is?' he suggested too coolly. 'And maybe we can work it out together. We're quite the capable team, you and I.'

Team? She actually quivered at being bracketed with him. So *stupid*. Of course she owed him the entire explanation. He'd just flown her to Vegas on her ill-tempered whim and she had to pull herself together. 'There's someone else involved.'

His grip hardened. '*Another* man? A different one from that other guy?'

She shook her head. 'Someone young and innocent. Someone who's lost enough already.'

'Meaning?'

She swallowed again because her throat was awfully tight. Just speaking about Lily upset Darcie. 'Her name is Lily. She's four years old and I'm going to foster her.'

'A child?' His eyes widened.

'My best friend's daughter.' She sighed. 'Zara died a few years ago and Lily's been in the system ever since.'

'She has no father around?'

'Not from the start.' Her words tumbled out. 'Lily's already been removed from one home. I can't let her face a future of constant upheaval…' It meant so much, touched nerves so raw she struggled to articulate it.

Elias's expression eased ever so slightly. 'You don't think there'll be other good foster parents?'

'There's no guarantee she'll get someone good and frankly there's no one as good as me.' Desperation shuddered through her and released in a volley of raw truth. '*I'm* here. *I* know her. *I* love her. And I can care for her better than *anyone* else ever could because I *know* what it's like!'

It took her a second to realise that not only had Elias stepped closer, but somehow she was basically leaning against him.

'You have a relationship with her.' The softest query.

'From the first.' Darcie couldn't bear to think of those years when she and Zara and lived together in their cramped, cold flat. 'Now I see her every Sunday unless I'm away, but even then I talk to her by phone. I refuse to disappear from her life and I will *never* stop fighting for her.' She drew breath and pushed back, pulling her wallet from her pocket she flipped it open so he could see the photo of Zara holding Lily. She needed to show him, to see his reaction.

He released her and remained still, the slightest of frowns knitting his brow as he studied the picture. Then he looked back up at her. She knew he was processing. *This* was the Elias she understood. Quick at comprehending. Quietly assessing all angles at lightning speed. Evaluating and deciding.

'But you've not been able to foster her until now,' he clarified.

Yeah, straight to the problem.

'They won't let me.' She dragged in another breath. 'At least they haven't until now. Apparently I was too young to apply to care full-time for a foster child when Zara died.'

There was a little more to it than that, but some things were too personal. Too mortifying.

'How long ago was that?'

'Just over three years,' she explained. 'Now I'm older but her latest social worker implied that being married will make me appear even more mature and capable of caring for her. That they'll think I'm less likely to ditch her and go clubbing.'

Bitterly she remembered the judgement of the case worker who'd come to see her the day Zara had died. The assumptions the woman had made when she'd seen where Zara and Darcie had lived. She'd instantly decided she'd never allow Darcie to keep caring for Lily. Darcie had had to fight hard to even stay in touch with the child.

'Clubbing? You?' Elias's gaze intensified. 'Have you ever gone clubbing?'

'Not in recent times,' she muttered, a cinder of embarrassment curling up from someplace buried deep.

'What else does this social worker suggest you need?'

'To be financially stable.'

'That's why you live in that place,' he muttered. 'You were saving all your money.'

'Yes.'

'But you can't raise a child in that tiny room.' He leapt to the next point. 'Where were you and whatshisname going to live? Does he have more of an apartment than you?'

'His flat is perfectly adequate.'

'Is it?' His mouth compressed into a flat line.

His scepticism made her defensiveness flare. 'We don't all need to live in a glass penthouse a stone's throw from Michelin restaurants and celebrity haunts. Some of us have more simple requirements.'

'Living within a stone's throw of Michelin restaurants isn't a necessity for a child,' he agreed. 'I'd have thought parks and peace would be more of a priority.'

'His flat was near a park.'

The muscle in his jaw flicked. 'So you need financial security, a good place to live and the appearance of stability in your personal life to enhance your application, do I have that correct?'

'It's the start, yes.' There would be interviews and assessment and monitoring but she would have the chance at least to prove that she could provide a loving home for Lily.

'I assume you'd need to present a happily married facade and demonstrate you're decent caregivers for the girl.'

'I would be the primary caregiver.'

'Of course.' He nodded. 'How long?'

'How long what?'

'For how long were you planning on being married to him?'

'Long enough for my foster care application to get approved. Possibly even made permanent.'

'That could take years.'

'We hadn't really nailed down a finish date. It was going to depend on how things worked out with the initial application.' She licked her lips. 'Of course there were going to be hoops.'

'The first of which was him sticking around for the wedding ceremony,' Elias said dryly.

The dart hit home. 'Shaun hasn't had it easy,' Darcie said defensively. 'I knew it was a big ask of him. But he would have gone through with it if you hadn't stormed in there like you owned—' She broke off and glared at him. 'Like you had any right to...'

'To what?'

'To follow me. To question me.' She flung her head back. 'To interfere with my life in *any* way.'

He was closer again now. 'He doesn't love you.'

So what? No one did. Almost no one ever had. Except for Zara. And Darcie loved Zara's daughter Lily like she was her own. She *was* family. The only one she had. 'And I already told you, marriage isn't always about love. And since when were you such a *romantic*? You don't care about anything other than your work. You'd never consider marriage. You're so cynical and controlled you—'

She broke off, realising how far over the mark she'd trod.

'Don't stop now, Darcie. Tell me how you really feel.'

How she *really* felt? About the hope she'd felt when he'd proposed—that it had been so selfishly centred? She shook her head and reminded herself of the basics. 'This isn't about that anymore. This is about Lily.'

Darcie ached to spare Lily the life both she and Zara had experienced.

He stared down at her. 'And you would do anything for her.'

'Yes.'

'Then why haven't you married me already? We could've been done five minutes ago.'

'Because you didn't know the whole story.'

'And now I do.'

'Yes, but—'

'Why the hesitation?' He suddenly frowned. 'Oh, I see, they've met Shaun. You turn up with a new groom now, you're going to look sketchy.'

'Actually, I hadn't told them yet.' She bit her lip. 'I wanted to make sure it was going to happen first.'

'You thought he might not come through for you?'

'I just wanted to be sure.'

'Can you be sure with me?'

She didn't know how to answer that.

His eyebrows shot up. 'You've been working for me for years. Do you not know me well enough to know you can count on me?' A sharp intake of breath. 'I've even brought you all the way here, Darcie. Now I'm really offended.'

'I didn't mean to offend you,' she mumbled. 'But it's not personal. I'm never sure about anyone.'

'No?' His gaze on her narrowed. 'Then be sure about this. I believe you've investigated all your options. You're highly intelligent and capable. If this is what you think you need, then my offer stands,' he said bluntly. 'You don't just need secure accommodation. You need a family home.' He listed off the requirements. 'You need financial security, space. If you would prefer not to work while you go through the system to get Lily, that's not a problem. I can provide all of these things for you.'

'But Lily needs more.' Darcie drew breath and faced reality—knowing it would make him change his mind. 'If you do this, then you'd be in her life. You'd have to have a relationship with her.'

'I wouldn't really be in her life.'

'You couldn't avoid her. Children pick up on—'

'I'm at work all day and I travel a lot. I'll be on the fringes. Her primary relationship is already with you. I would only pop in here and there.'

Something made her doggedly deny this would be that easy. 'If you didn't really want her, she would know. She would feel it. '

His mouth thinned. 'I would want her to be happy and secure. She would understand that. Did you have concerns about this with your previous groom?'

'Shaun loved Zara and I knew he would love Lily because of that.' She lifted her chin. 'But you don't believe in love. And apparently you don't believe in marriage without love. Ergo, you don't believe in marriage.' She questioned him. 'So *why* would you do this? Why would you even *want* to?'

He gazed beyond her for a moment and then looked back. His blue eyes cooler, sharper somehow. 'Because there are advantages to my getting married. Especially to someone like you.'

'Like *me*?' She stiffened. What did he mean by that?

'We have much in common,' he said. 'Neither of us is ruled by excessive emotion. At least—' a rueful smile curved his mouth '—not usually. We're able to recognise a good deal and we both understand the sacrifices needed to make sure it happens. We can coolly work through the benefits and the costs of any kind of arrangement.'

The benefits and the costs? Darcie shivered at his clinical assessment of their commonalities, and in reality he was wrong.

She'd had no real choice other than to keep her cool in the office. And if she had a real choice now she'd stomp out of here in a heartbeat. Only the thought of Lily kept her back. And okay, *he* kept her back. Her desire for them *both*.

'You're able to suppress your appetite and emotions in the business environment. You have extraordinary control, Darcie. It's admirable.'

'It's not some admirable strength, Elias,' she said harshly. 'It was a necessity.'

'Because you needed the job. You needed the money.'

'Yes.'

'Even so, plenty of people couldn't cope the way you did. They'd get another job. You didn't. You stayed. You were determined to, I think.'

She lifted her chin. Yes, there was that. She hadn't wanted to be bettered by him. He was the challenge and she'd revelled in rising to his requirements and never letting him know how close to the edge she really was. But long term it was unsustainable because of how she really felt.

Something gleamed in his eyes. 'You're a match for me, Darcie. And I won't deny the appearance of stability in my personal life would be advantageous for me at this time.'

Elias Greyson liked to win and he was very used to it. But this particular challenge was one he now wanted with a need that sliced bone deep. But she'd been dependent upon him for her job and only now did he understand why she'd so desperately needed that income. That power imbalance had prevented her from being completely honest—perhaps even completely herself—with him. And here he was setting himself up for more of the same, was he not? Because her *gratitude* to this marriage could constrain her behaviour. He was going to have to be careful, ensure they fully communicated. He was going to have to keep this controlled. But recapturing his usual cool clarity was challenging because there was one last piece of the Darcie puzzle he'd yet to properly solve. While there were still shadows and secrets in her eyes, some things she couldn't hide, and that included the very basic, very strong, chemistry sparking between them. And suddenly all that mattered—the urge overriding reason—was that she did not walk out the way she'd walked out this morning. The next time she left him it would be on his terms and at a time of his choosing.

'You said not all marriages are for romance or based in love. They're a solution to a problem,' he said harshly.

She didn't move. 'Yes, but I still don't understand what problem you face. This would be a huge imposition—an awfully big sacrifice for you to make.'

That this all *was* about a child had made him feel both better and worse. He didn't want to think of Darcie pregnant by some other man. Yeah, it was an appalling gut reaction—he'd no right to feel possessive or jealous. Yet he had.

'You don't think I'm capable of making a sacrifice for someone?'

Colour flooded her face. 'No, that's not what I meant.'

'Sure it was,' he said softly. Offended all over again.

Surely he was a better bet than the jerk who'd walked out on her only moments before their wedding?

'But you're still not grasping the advantage

for me,' he said more calmly than he was feeling. 'This would be convenient.'

'Convenient?'

The flight had bought him time to consider the pros and cons of joining forces with Darcie on a more permanent basis and the more he'd thought about it, the more sense it had made. She'd been right in that he didn't believe in marriage, but marriage could be viewed as simply another merger. Political alliances dating back hundreds of years, across all cultures had succeeded. Without confusion or complications, they worked. And although he certainly didn't believe a couple should stay together for a child, the point here was he and Darcie *wouldn't* stay together. It was only until Lily's guardianship was awarded to Darcie that the arrangement needed to last.

The thought of that child being lonely and scared in an unsafe place was untenable. It hadn't been often for Elias, but he had felt unsafe at times. And while Elias had never wanted to be a father—he knew he didn't have the skills—he didn't hate children. And the thought of this one orphaned and alone made his gut ache. A child needed and deserved to be wanted. And Lily was. By Darcie. But it was more than the thought of Lily driving him now. It was the expression in Darcie's eyes when she'd described the little girl's situation, and her desire to be there, that compelled him. *Her* heartbreak.

He ached to ease it for her. More than that, there was a fierce, irrational drive to keep her close.

Not irrational. It was pure basic instinct. He'd not acknowledged to himself before how much he wanted her because he'd had to push it away. It had been inappropriate and out of bounds. But now?

'I don't do love, Darcie, but it seems you understand that already,' he suddenly snapped. 'You're not in love with me, correct?'

'Correct,' Darcie instinctively snapped back.

'Then this is nothing more than another deal. After a year we'll understand the likelihood of success in your application to care for the child. We'll review the arrangement then.'

She blinked. He'd give her one whole year to try for Lily. 'Why would you want a wife for a year?'

'Why wouldn't I?' he countered. 'Especially a wife who understands the pressures of my work upon my time. A woman who understands my lifestyle. A wife will give me the air of humanity I'm often accused of lacking and a beautiful wife is the one thing I currently don't have as a societal measure of success.'

A *beautiful* wife? She shook her head as she

realised how out of her depth she was. 'I'm not the sort of wife you should have.'

To her amazement he actually smiled. 'In what way could you possibly be deficient?'

She rolled her eyes. 'I'm not well-educated. I didn't go to the right schools and know all the right people. I don't have the required etiquette. I'm not a clothes model. I'll embarrass you.' There. A matter-of-fact assessment of her shortcomings. Not *quite* all of them, but the only ones she was prepared to articulate now.

'I don't want a model wife,' he said bluntly. 'I want someone who understands what I do and how much it matters to me. Someone who can fit in with minimal disruption. And, yes, I'm aware you're bringing a child with you but your demands upon me won't be those of a normal wife because we already understand that this is going to be a business relationship. My benefit is knowing I'll no longer be judged for dating or for my lifestyle.'

'But you don't care what anyone says about you,' she pointed out, equally bluntly.

'I care when it impacts on my deals.' He lifted his chin. 'And Vince Williams doesn't like my lifestyle.'

So it really was only for business.

'After the end of our brief marriage, I will, naturally, be devastated and vow never to marry again. Perhaps people will finally consider I have a valid reason to remain single.'

'That's preposterous.'

'Yet enchantingly believable.' He actually smiled again. 'People will think it serves me right. You'll have to be the villainess who breaks my formerly impenetrable heart, Darcie. Can you cope with the momentary vilification or shall you not care?'

'No one will ever believe I broke your heart. People will perceive it to be the other way round.'

'And will you cope with that?'

She straightened. 'Of course, because I'll have Lily and I really don't care what anyone says about me. And this is just a pretence.'

'Exactly. A pretence that serves an admirably worthy goal.'

Yet she still couldn't quite say yes. There was still one thing they had to address. 'What would you expect of me personally?' She braced when she saw a flicker of amusement around his mouth. 'Do you expect we'll be intimate?'

He shot her a coolly devastating look. 'You weren't averse to the idea of being intimate with me a couple of weeks ago, Darcie.'

Yeah, it had been inevitable that he would point that mortifying fact out.

'Why did you do it?' He finally asked the

question that had been hanging between them for days. 'Why did you proposition me that night in Edinburgh?'

Darcie swallowed, buying time even when she'd had days to dream up some flippant reply. But she had none. She had to be honest, because apparently the man was seriously still willing to give her the chance to get almost everything she wanted.

'You were planning to marry someone else,' he added when she didn't immediately reply. 'I assume you were engaged at the time you asked me back to your room?'

'Yes.'

'You would have cheated on him.'

She shook her head. 'It wasn't a real engagement and it wasn't going to be a real wedding. We weren't going to...' She huffed the tightness from her chest. 'I wasn't going to sleep with Shaun. We don't have that kind of relationship.'

'Really?' Elias's eyes narrowed. 'You're what, *friends*?'

She didn't know why he sounded so sceptical. 'Is that so hard to believe? We were in the same group home for a while.'

'Group home?'

'Foster homes,' she explained.

'Why was Shaun doing it then?'

Darcie hesitated. She was unsure of what Elias's reaction would be to the fact that she'd given Shaun money. So she opted for partial truth. 'I told you he loved Lily's mother, my friend Zara. He was doing it for her.'

'Not because he wanted you?'

'No.' She braced again. 'Aside from the fact that he told you, isn't it obvious given how quickly he abandoned me when you showed up and started raging?'

Elias's frown only deepened. 'So you weren't going to sleep with him at all through the marriage?'

'I wasn't going to sleep with *anyone*.'

'But that night you decided the engagement didn't count and you thought you'd try me? Did you want one last romp before you sacrificed your sex life so you could foster your friend's daughter?'

She felt a blush burning its way up her entire body. She'd thought it her one chance for *any* kind of sex life. 'I guess you could put it that way.'

'How else would you put it?' He leaned closer. 'Explain it to me, Darcie. Why, when you've worked for me for years, did you suddenly decide to proposition me out of the blue?'

'I knew I was leaving and you weren't going to be my boss anymore, and I got a little drunk and I was...' She rolled her shoulders. She'd hoped he'd forgotten those five minutes of pure mortification, but she couldn't explain the last part. It was *too* personal. 'It doesn't matter anyway. You didn't want me. Nothing happened aside from me making a massive fool of myself.'

'I didn't want you?'

'Obviously not.'

'Obviously?' He was like a statue again. 'You knew I couldn't possibly say yes.'

She stared at him sceptically. He never said no to other women. He had short flings all the time. Sometimes it had felt like he'd sleep with anyone *but* her.

'You were tipsy,' he gritted. 'I'd watched you. You'd had three glasses of champagne when you never normally drink a drop.'

Well, yes. She'd been drowning her sorrows and crazy courage had surged in their place.

'Moreover, and more importantly,' he rasped, 'I was your boss. There was a power imbalance—one that had been there from the moment we met.'

'But I was leaving.'

'I didn't know that then,' he shot back.

But it wouldn't have made any difference. She'd humiliated herself. 'I'm sorry I put you in an awkward position.'

'An awkward position?' He echoed in disbelief. 'You have no idea what position you put me in that night.'

Heat scorched her face.

'Darcie Milne. Assistant extraordinaire.'

Bitterness rose. 'You didn't want to lose me as an assistant.' She wasn't a *woman* to him. She didn't think he'd ever seen her as one.

'No. I was never going to risk losing my best assistant.'

'But then I resigned.' Could she sound any more desperate?

'Until this morning I was confident I could get you to change your mind and stay.'

She blinked. She thought he'd forgotten or simply didn't care that she'd resigned. But how had he planned to change her mind? 'Because you're good at convincing women to do whatever you want them to?'

'I've never treated you in that way.'

Yes. Didn't she know it.

'And I certainly wasn't going to take advantage of you at the time,' he said.

'Because I was tipsy and you were my boss.'

'Yes,' he growled impatiently.

'Is there any situation in which you would take advantage of me?'

Somehow the shocking question slid out. There was a silence. And mortification. All over again.

'I *never* want to take advantage of you,' he said.

Of course it was the right answer. So why did that teeny tiny part of her feel crushed?

'I would far prefer to have you as my equal, Darcie. Where one of us doesn't take advantage of the other.'

'We're *never* going to be equals, Elias.' He had too much power. 'We're too different—our backgrounds, education, everything.'

'I disagree. I think we could be equal in curiosity, integrity and loyalty and we could even be equal in this marriage. If it goes ahead, I wouldn't want you breaking your vows to me and I won't break mine to you.'

'You'll survive a sexless life?'

Something flickered in his face. 'It's only one year, is it not?' He stepped closer. 'If this happens then this lingering power imbalance between us has to be gone. As my wife, you're not *required* to do anything. Certainly not sleep with me. Though—' Laughter suddenly flashed in his eyes. 'You might actually have to dine with me on occasion. And engage with my clients in a capacity that straddles the business and the personal.'

She gazed up at him, knowing she should say yes, yet something still held her back. 'You don't really need me for any of that. It's still not much of a win for you.'

'Perhaps it's the most simple win of all. The intangible, altruistic satisfaction of doing something for someone else.'

Her heart thudded hard then. 'For Lily.'

'Right,' he nodded. 'For Lily.'

That's when she got lost in his eyes, trying to understand the man she'd thought she knew.

His lips compressed and he glanced at the clock on the wall. 'We don't have much longer, Darcie. You need to decide.'

But her brain was oddly sluggish. She'd seen Zara try the 'love' route and it had ended in disaster. Playing on old loyalties and emotions—like what she'd tried with Shaun—hadn't worked either. A cool businesslike contract? Maybe that was the answer.

She'd known all her life that people couldn't be trusted. Ultimately—always—they left. Both her parents had left her. Zara had left her. Shaun had just left her. Elias would, too, eventually. But he wasn't promising forever. He wasn't promising any kind of frills. He was being upfront about the facts. This wasn't just a fake marriage; it was a short-term one. And she knew Elias. He was ruthless but he was also fair. She *had* seen him follow through on deal after deal. She'd seen him have high expectations of people's performance but he'd also rewarded those who deserved it. Including her. Maybe she could trust him to maintain his side of this bargain.

She understood that he would be absent a lot. But if she were successful at getting her placement, Darcie would be Lily's primary caregiver, and one person could make all the difference in another's life. You could have a big family and feel nothing but lonely and isolated. Or worse. Sometimes you needed just *one* person. Lily needed her.

She searched Elias's face. She had no idea what kind of family he'd come from or even whether he was in touch with any of them. Did he have siblings? Where were his parents? In almost three years there'd been no reference to them at all. What would they think of this? But if he wasn't concerned, then she shouldn't be either, right?

And if there was no emotion between them, maybe there'd be no real expectations that neither of them could live up to.

'Well?' he prompted, his customary curtness restored.

It was enough to solidify her thinking. This was her last chance. He wasn't going to repeat it, or wait for her to think about it long. She knew how he operated. Once he made an offer, the clock started ticking. Accept quickly or miss out forever.

'Okay.' Courage slammed into her veins. 'Let's get married. Right now.'

CHAPTER SIX

ELIAS'S SUDDEN SMILE was a dazzling flash of pure triumph that Darcie hadn't expected. But he turned away so abruptly she could hardly absorb let alone enjoy it. She dragged in a breath as he went out of the room and called something to the receptionist. The man was even more incredible when he smiled, and that wasn't often enough.

'Would you prefer gold or platinum for your wedding ring?' he asked when he returned. 'You can choose a fine or a heavier set band.'

Darcie blinked at the small collection of gleaming silver and gold rings in the sleek box he'd pulled from his pocket. 'Did you bring this from your collection?'

She knew he kept a supply of jewellery. The first time he'd cancelled a date early on in her employment she'd assumed he'd ask her to arrange a flower delivery or some such, but when she'd offered to do just that—in an attempt to demonstrate her ability to anticipate his needs— he'd looked miffed and coolly informed her that he dealt with his own personal messes, particularly 'clean-up' operations. He'd bluntly added that she wasn't paid to be some kind of emotional nanny. That's when she'd seen the stash in his office safe. 'Clean-up' clearly meant 'pay-off'. He had to have a subscription service to a top jewellery house so he'd always have something appropriate to give a date on any occasion—from the first date to final farewell. At the time she'd almost admired his cold-blooded, richer-than-rich efficiency. But today his practical, clinical planning annoyed her.

'No,' he said blandly. 'The driver collected them from a jeweller on his way to pick us up. Choose one, and if it doesn't fit properly we'll have it adjusted back in London.'

Darcie just pointed to the first one.

'Do you wish to vary the vows or use their standard template?' he asked, his smile audible.

'Standard template is fine,' she muttered mechanically.

'And we'll just stay as we are clothing-wise.' He glanced at the clock on the wall. 'Two minutes and it's our turn. Are my organisational efforts almost at Darcie Milne standards?'

'Almost,' she said stiffly.

Three minutes later it was almost over.

To have and hold... For better. Worse. Richer. Poorer. Sickness. Health. To love...always.

The words on the small tablet the marriage celebrant held seemed to float in space in front of her. That she was audible was a shock. More shocking was that faint smile seemingly glued to Elias's face. That he was doing this at all astounded her, but that he was amused by it?

Her heart galloped as anticipation burgeoned. They were going to kiss. Actually kiss. Because now they were husband and wife and the celebrant was looking at them expectantly and there was a skinny teenager holding up a camera.

She froze, breathless, as expectation built to unbearable levels. Elias leaned close. So close. Her eyes drifted shut. The brush of his lips on hers was gossamer light. So light and cool and yet there was an infinitesimal hit of—

He lifted away. He was gone and it had lasted less than a second.

Darcie's eyes flashed open. She stared—shocked and dismayed—because her disappointment was catastrophic. And for a far longer moment than that paltry 'kiss' he looked right at her with an intense, but inscrutable, expression.

'Right,' he suddenly snapped. 'Let's go.'

Darcie nodded, unable to answer.

She was so *stupid*. He hadn't wanted her two weeks ago and he hadn't wanted her now, either—not the way *she* wanted. That 'kiss' had merely been the symbolic, societally required confirmation of their *deal*, not a demonstration of undeniable lust.

Mortified, she wondered what hell she'd just

thrown herself into. Because she ached for the man who was now her husband in name only and she had the horrible feeling he'd just seen that. She *had* to pull herself together.

'Do we go straight back to the airport?' she asked desperately.

'We do.' He walked with her to the waiting limousine.

'Good. I need to get back to London as soon as possible.'

There wasn't going to be a honeymoon. That five-minute marriage ceremony meant nothing more than a means to an end. She shouldn't feel this crushed.

'*After* the meeting for the Williams acquisition,' he said.

Oh, right. She'd forgotten that. She scrunched into the far corner of the back seat and pulled out her phone to distract herself. He'd done the same, was firing off message after message. Keeping the company running, no doubt.

'You're worried about Lily?' Elias asked after a few moments, his face still focused on his screen. 'Don't be. I'll get the legal team on it right away.'

The awful thing was she'd hadn't thought about Lily at all in the last few minutes. She'd been thinking only about *herself*. Now she focused. Lily needed her. And then she remembered Shaun.

'Darcie?' Elias's query was soft yet commanding. 'Is everything okay?'

She'd been so fixated on wanting him to touch her she'd forgotten everything that was far more important. Now she willed a message to ping on her phone. But there was nothing. *Hell.* She had to face the reality that the bulk of the independent funds she'd accumulated for herself was all but gone. It wasn't as if she'd never been let down before. But it was embarrassing to have it all happen in front of Elias, who was always so together and who simply wouldn't stand for such treatment. She didn't want to tell him. She didn't want his pity, or his anger, she wanted another kind of attention altogether. She wanted his—

'Is there something more I ought to know?' Elias pressed. 'You look…'

She didn't want him to look at her. She didn't want him to see anything she was truly thinking. Maybe it was better to admit one embarrassment over a far more brutally personal one. 'It's Shaun,' she said baldly.

'What about him?' Elias almost bristled.

Yes. It was a good distraction. 'I need to get in touch with him.'

'Because?'

'Because I gave him money to set up his business and I need to make sure the deal has gone through.'

'You gave him money? When?' Elias's eyes widened. 'Darcie, did you *pay* him to marry you?'

'It was a business arrangement, not so different to this one, really.'

'But he's taken the money and run without delivering his end of the deal,' he said curtly. 'How *much*, Darcie?'

What did it matter? 'As I said, he needed money to invest in his business. I wanted to help and I was going to oversee the accounting once it was underway. If he'd made it a success it would've been good for us.' She saw Elias's expression turn thunderous. 'It's my fault, not his.'

But she'd really thought Shaun had it together. Bitter embarrassment surged. 'I bet you're wishing you'd pushed for more from me now, huh. Knowing I was desperate enough to pay someone almost everything I have.'

'Almost everything?' Elias couldn't believe what he was hearing. 'How much did you transfer to him? When?'

She couldn't look at him as she told him and he couldn't look away from her. He'd scarcely been able to look away from her since that moment in front of the celebrant—when he'd very determinedly not kissed her again; when he'd seen her reaction; when he'd felt terrible.

Now he felt worse. Because now he registered how pale she'd grown. There were smudges beneath her eyes and her mouth drooped. She was exhausted—not just physically, but emotionally, and for the first time since that first job interview she looked fragile.

'That's a lot of money.' Elias battled the urge to pull her close and make her lean on him. Instead he forced himself to look away and focus on the scenery out the window. The afternoon was closing. It would be late by the time they finally arrived in San Francisco. Too late to talk through what they'd just done. And he had a million things to organise. 'You saved all that from working with me?'

'I didn't have a lot to spend it on.'

'Not that you chose to,' he countered.

But maybe it wasn't that material things didn't interest her...she'd just had to make choices. Plus, she'd had little time to spend money on experiences because she was always working for him. So yeah, no wonder she'd been able to save so much.

'My goal has always been Lily. To do everything I can for her,' she confirmed his thinking. 'If I couldn't become her caregiver then I planned to pay for her to go a good school. I hoped they'd agree. I thought that would have given her stability in that way at least.'

He couldn't resist trying to slake just some of his curiosity. 'Did you go to a good school?'

She shot him a startled look. 'What? No.'

But she was very bright. He knew she could have aced any scholarship exams but he suspected she'd never been given the chance. Why was that? How long had she been in the foster system? Because she had been. She knew 'what it was like'. The injustice of it burned. Her focus was fully fixed on giving her friend's daughter a better life than either she or her friend had had. But what about her own life—her dreams for *herself*? What had those been? What were they now?

His curiosity burned hotter—and most intensely—about her personal desires. Because he'd seen the awareness in her eyes as he'd approached in that sparse, speedy ceremony. He'd felt the receptive softness of her lips. He'd instinctively pulled away. *Immediately.* He'd had to end it—making it the most minimal of kisses. But he couldn't have the first time he kissed her properly be in front of costumed strangers complete with camera in hand. He'd ached for privacy and space.

But then he'd seen her face. He'd seen the yearning and the disappointment. That's when he'd truly understood the depth of her desire. And he was yet to get his heart back to its normal rhythm.

Want, right? Pure, physical want. Still now, even as they were driven back to the plane, he fought the irresistible urge to press her luscious body to his. He wanted to plunder. He wanted everything here and now and it had never been as impossible. Because she was exhausted. So exhausted.

So he had to ignore that unbearable, hungry ache running the length of him. He couldn't quite believe the events of the day—couldn't yet figure why he'd reacted to such an extreme. He'd *married* her. Yet what he was discovering today challenged everything he'd thought he knew. Emotionless Darcie? That couldn't be further from the truth. And she was nowhere near as immune to him as she'd been acting for these last two years. He'd known that—but not the degree of her interest.

He battled the urge to reach for her hand. If they were to kiss again, it had to happen in privacy. It had to happen when there was the time and space to do *everything*. Because if it happened again there would be no stopping. But it couldn't happen at all until she was ready.

Until she *said*. And that was never going to be tonight.

Darcie followed Elias back into the waiting jet.

'The flight to San Francisco isn't long,' he

said almost bracingly. 'It'll be better to get there tonight so we'll be fresh for tomorrow.'

'Do you really need me to attend the dinner?'

'You know Vince Williams has strong views. If he hears I've got married—and doubtless he will—then he'll deeply disapprove of my not bringing you.'

'I really don't know that I can project the image you're going for,' she muttered.

'You don't think you can look happy to be married to me?' He shuddered. 'Darcie, you devastate me.'

She rolled her eyes as she fastened her seatbelt. 'I just don't see how it's going to be believable.'

'Why not?' he asked.

There was chemistry that was obvious between a couple, wasn't there? And there clearly wasn't any on his side. She was still smarting from that no-nonsense, barely happened kiss. She gripped the armrests and braced through the take-off and kept her mouth firmly shut.

'We can say we kept our affair under wraps for a long time,' he said when the plane finally levelled out. 'What with the sticky issue of you being my employee until today.'

'What about the fact that your other employees all knew I was getting married and that it *wasn't* to you,' she couldn't resist pointing out. 'It's going to cause a huge gossipy scandal.'

'At your job interview with me you told me you weren't there to make friends, but to get the job done,' he said. 'But it wasn't true. You were friends with them. You told them about your wedding.'

'I hadn't intended to. It slipped out the night before.'

'At the dinner you didn't invite me to.'

'You wouldn't have attended even if I'd asked you. It's not what you do.'

'Dinner isn't what you do either,' he pointed out. 'But it was only pizza, right?'

She stared at him, startled. Because yes, it had been exactly that. Pizza when they were all standing at a bar, not even at a table.

Then his smile suddenly appeared. 'Given that I stormed out of the office after you this morning, I think they'll spin it as some great romantic story—'

'You what?'

'I was too shocked to think.'

'Shocked that I was getting married?' she asked, stung.

'No. Because I thought you were...' He frowned. 'Cheating or something.'

Oh. 'That really pushed your buttons,' she said softly.

'I was so angry I couldn't tell you what I was thinking.'

It had been strong emotional response. Though she knew it wasn't *her* he'd responded to, but the situation. The fact he thought she was cheating. He'd felt for her *groom*, right? Plus, he'd been annoyed that she'd walked out on him. Elias was used to getting what he wanted. But maybe he hadn't always in the past.

They were married. Surely they now needed to learn some personal things about each other—at least to project the illusion of being happily married. 'Have you…had experience with how horrible it is to go through that? To be betrayed by someone?'

His expression shuttered. 'I've seen the fall-out from an affair—I know how bad it can be.' He cleared his throat. 'But anyway, all my employees are paid extremely well. Their contract includes discretion. They won't sell us out. Not if they want to keep their jobs.'

He was probably right. And he hadn't wanted to explain anything more about whatever— whoever—that affair was. She got it. She didn't like considering her past much either. And that thought made her realise another danger.

'Shaun might,' she said.

'Shaun might,' he agreed. 'But then he's not going to look very good in it, is he? Especially when he still has the money you transferred to him.'

Yeah. She'd tried to buy a husband. She'd tried to play on Shaun's feelings for Zara. It wasn't that he and she were that close. And she hadn't had anyone else to call on. No family—she'd never had that. No friends—because she'd lost Zara. And since that terrible moment, she'd been working—striving towards getting Lily. It cut deep to realise yet again how alone she was. She didn't want Lily to be alone the way she was. She wanted to build a better life for them both.

She tried not to pay attention when Elias unfastened his seatbelt and moved to the rear of the compartment. She had to get back to not looking at him too much again. But then he appeared right back in front of her. He'd rolled up his sleeves and she couldn't help drinking in the sight of his strong forearms. She knew he went to the gym to work out, but those muscles and that tan suggested outdoor activity as well. He was long, lean and strong and bending towards her and she wanted him to—

'Oh.' She bit her lip.

'I don't believe you're not hungry, Darcie.'

'This looks amazing.' She hurriedly gestured towards the fresh platter he was holding. 'There's always cheese in the office,' she added inanely, desperately trying to cover that embarrassing moment. 'Actually, there are all kinds of snacks in there.'

'Yes.'

She narrowed her gaze suspiciously because that purring answer didn't sound benign. An odd thought occurred. There hadn't always been snacks. Not at the beginning. The other assistants had commented on it when they started appearing. Her heat began to rise.

'Did you…' She trailed off and shook her head. That was a *stupid* thought. All of a sudden she was reading everything into nothing.

'Did I what?' He retook his seat and then gazed across at her with that amusement glinting more visibly in his eyes. 'Did I order all those snacks that are in the office especially for you? Why yes, Darcie, I did.'

Especially for her? She gaped. 'Why would you do that?'

No one had done that—not thought of her tastes, not done something solely for her—in ages. Not since Zara. They'd have done anything for each other, and Darcie would do just that for Zara's daughter. Literally anything. Even marry a man she didn't love.

'Why wouldn't I?' Elias asked casually. 'You function best when you're not starving.'

She bristled. 'I have *never* not functioned well.'

Nor had she starved. Well, not really.

His amused expression deepened. 'That's not what I said. I meant that your performance is *optimal* when you're properly fuelled. Though how you can never seem to manage an actual meal is beyond me. But you like to snack on small plates interspersed throughout the day and that's fine. It is in the company's best interests to supply you with them.'

'The *company's* best interests?'

'Fine. Mine. As I basically am the company. So I guess I really mean me.'

'I guess you do,' she said huskily.

She was astounded he'd even noticed her habits, let alone surreptitiously *supplied* her preferences. But he'd not told her. Not until now. Why? Didn't he want her to think he was actually kind? Too bad. She already knew he was. She'd seen him do things in an annoyingly abrupt way for others—he was thoughtful, yet sandpaperish at the same time. It was those barriers of his, she realised.

'Thank you,' she said softly. Her flush built. It wasn't something she was used to saying because people didn't often do things for her.

He was watching her too closely. 'It was my pleasure.'

Her pulse pounded. It was a courteous reply. He didn't mean it in an *intimate* way. Except his voice was gravelly and the heat in the cabin had increased even more.

'Now will you please enjoy it?' He gestured to the platter.

But she nibbled only a little because strangely her appetite still hadn't made an appearance. It wasn't anxiety; it was hotter than that. 'What about you?'

'I'm enjoying watching you.'

Again there was that thread of something that shouldn't be there. That she couldn't really have heard. She was tired, right? Hearing things he wasn't intending. Except she wasn't all that tired anymore. When she ought to be exhausted, she was growing more alert by the second. But Elias turned to his computer, apparently content to work on the journey for once. That was on her; she'd stolen his time.

They finally landed and were driven to the hotel in the heart of San Francisco. Darcie's breath got shorter, her awareness more intense.

'We have the penthouse suite,' Elias muttered to her as the concierge deferentially stepped forward to greet him.

Darcie lost her stomach in the lift as it whisked them to the top of the building. She heard the beep as the door unlocked and she stepped forward into the suite. There was a large lounge with stunning views across the skyline and several doors leading from the vestibule. Elias walked to the nearest and opened it. Darcie stilled.

He glanced back from the threshold. 'Good night, Darcie. Sleep well.'

Stunned, she watched him close the door behind him.

He'd left her alone. On automatic pilot, she walked to another door. The bedroom was stunning—luxurious and peaceful—but it didn't soothe the resentment that had suddenly soared. It was her wedding night and she was lying alone in an enormous bed. An unclaimed virgin bride. She'd married a man she knew to have a 'healthy' appetite towards sex. A billionaire playboy no less.

But even he didn't want her.

CHAPTER SEVEN

DARCIE HAD DECIDED the easiest thing would be to work. To pretend they weren't actually husband and wife. Elias, however, had other ideas.

'What do you mean you don't want me to help you prepare for the meeting?' She glared at him across the dining table in their suite. It was littered with toast, fruit, pastries and a coffeepot, all of which they were both ignoring.

She'd taken so long to get to sleep that by the time she finally had, she was so exhausted she'd entered deep sleep mode and then actually slept in far later than usual. Now it was almost ten thirty and Elias was due for the first of his meetings at Williams VC headquarters.

But apparently he wasn't in a hurry to leave. He shook his head. 'Everything is done. The last report I needed has come in from London. You can relax here and take your time getting ready for tonight.'

Take her time getting ready? What was he expecting?

She bit her lip. The *last* thing she wanted was several hours in which to grow even more nervous. She'd basically been working all the hours of all her adult life and frankly didn't have much socialising experience. Faking it behind a clip-board was one thing. Having to front up and engage not just with other people, but with *him*, was a challenge.

'I'll re-read the report on Williams and his wife in readiness,' she said.

'You wrote the report, didn't you?' He eyed her with amusement.

She had. And she knew its contents. So obviously there were other ways in which to 'get ready'. 'What should I wear then?'

A wary look entered his eyes. 'Should you wear?'

She drummed her fingers on the table between them. 'I don't normally attend business dinners with you.'

'Because you never wanted to. You always said you had paperwork to attend to.'

'Right. But this time I'm required and you'll be introducing me as your wife.' She gestured towards her white blouse and grey trousers. 'So is my usual outfit suitable or do I need to dress more like...' She shifted uncomfortably. 'More like one of your dates.'

'What do you think my dates normally wear?' His mouth twitched.

Not much, from what she'd seen in the photos that splashed across social media and 'celebrity spy' sites. Because they often were celebrities.

Socialites. Models. Actresses. Savvy influencer entrepreneurs. He'd dated a bunch of gorgeous women who weren't afraid of being seen. And judged. *Not* something Darcie was confident with.

'Glamorous strappy dresses,' she said.

'You'd prefer not to wear one of those?'

She wouldn't know where to buy one, plus now she couldn't really afford one and yes, she had major doubts as to how good she'd look in one. 'What would people expect your wife to wear?'

She just had to make it to passable; perfection was obviously out of the question.

'I don't know about other people, but *I'd* expect my wife to wear whatever makes *her* feel comfortable. Don't wear something you don't like because you think you have to. Wear whatever you want.' He glanced at her speculatively. 'Just as you are is more than adequate, Darcie.'

More than adequate? Her irritation mushroomed.

'Of course, given you had little time to pack anything else yesterday, you might choose to shop for something new,' he then added thoughtfully. 'And if you did want to do that, then I'd expect you to use my account. After all, this dinner is effectively a work meeting. But you don't have to if you don't want. It's your choice.'

He held her gaze captive. 'Everything is your choice, Darcie.'

There was a seductive edge to his voice that made her shiver. She tensed. She couldn't embarrass herself all over again. She'd literally offered herself to him once already and he wasn't interested. What he'd said yesterday—about not being able to take up her offer because he was her boss—that was just a line. He couldn't have made it more clear that even though he was now her husband, he wasn't interested. He'd bestowed a micro-kiss on her at the altar before bundling her out of that wedding chapel and got them back on his plane as fast as was humanly possible. Then he'd all but broken his neck to get himself into a separate bedroom from her. While she was exhausted because she'd not been able to sleep at all, he, drat him, looked well rested and more gorgeous than ever.

Didn't he have *any* concerns about what they'd done? Didn't he have anyone else he even ought to tell? But she'd worked alongside him for years and, while there was much she knew because of that, there were so many things she didn't. Important things.

'Won't your family wonder about you getting married in such a rush?' she asked recklessly. 'Won't your parents think it's random?'

He poured himself a coffee. 'I'm not close to my parents.'

'You're not going to tell them?' She stilled.

'I'm sure they'll find out. But not from me.'

'Won't they wonder if—'

'I don't care about other people's speculation.'

But they weren't talking about other people. They were talking about his *parents*. She watched as he pulled some papers closer. Back to work? *Really?*

'You don't care about anything much as long as it doesn't impact on the business,' she said slowly.

'That's right.' He glanced up, his tone unapologetic. 'And my taking on a wife and a foster child certainly isn't going to look bad for the business.'

'But if you don't care, then you really don't need us to rehabilitate your image so people think you're actually human.'

He suddenly laughed. 'Am I all cold-blooded capitalist, Darcie? Maybe you're right. I must admit I spent most of last night trying to figure out just how I ended up here.'

'Temporary insanity?' she suggested.

'I think partly it was because it was the *last* thing you expected of me. I enjoyed confounding you.'

She stiffened, a little annoyed. Because yeah.

She'd seen that. 'You've landed yourself with a whole lot of trouble just for the momentary thrill of one-upping me.'

His smile turned wolfish. 'Who says the thrill is momentary?'

Awareness prickled, followed by a lurching desire to provoke something more from him again. She looked down and fiddled with the coffee cup. 'Fortunately for you, our marriage isn't consummated. It's not too late to get an annulment.'

The silence stretched. Ultimately Darcie couldn't resist it. She had to look back up at him.

Elias was simply staring at her and Darcie found that not only could she not move, she couldn't breathe. She gazed back, amazed at the swirling depth of emotion in his eyes. He usually kept that masked. Kept it contained. But there had to be an outlet for it sometime, right?

Beautiful women in strappy dresses.

'Darcie, you know me well enough to understand that I'm not someone who quits,' he said softly. 'Not ever. We're in this together until we win.'

Were they? She wasn't sure what the prize was anymore.

'Actually, I do have something I'd like you to wear tonight if you're so inclined.' He reached into his pocket and put a box on the table. 'A little material possession for you.'

Another jewellery box. Was it another item from his collection of emergency pacifiers for problematic dates he wanted to detach himself of? 'Trophy of *your* possession, you mean?' she asked acidly.

'You were concerned about believability.' His eyes glittered as he opened the box. 'And people will never believe that a man as wealthy I wouldn't bestow a trinket upon my bride.'

'A *trinket*…that's what you call this?'

'What would you call it?'

'Ostentatious.'

She refused to appreciate the stunning piece. This meant nothing to him. This was money he didn't know what else to do with.

He took her hand and she battled the instinctive tremble.

'I like that it can be seen from a hundred feet. It makes it fit for purpose.' He slowly slid the sparkling diamond solitaire down her finger. 'You're the one who wanted this.'

'Not *this*.'

'Not all the finer points?' he queried. 'You hadn't thought everything through?' He shook his head. 'That doesn't seem like you, Darcie. You're a details person. But in this it seems you were just going to wing it.'

And he was teasing her for that by going full out with everything she'd basically forgotten. Or chosen not to consider. A brief kiss at the altar. An engagement ring. Things she hadn't been going to have at all. But that now she discovered that she wanted. Desperately.

But not a wedding night.

'Isn't it fortunate you always have jewellery on hand,' she said tartly.

'I've never needed an engagement ring before.' That smile in his eyes deepened. 'I had to go to a jeweller first thing this morning and choose it myself with only you in mind.'

She gritted her teeth.

'So there's no need to be jealous, Darcie,' he added lightly. 'You're my wife, and as such you're the *only* woman I'll give jewels to henceforth.'

'I'm not—'

'Hard as you might find it to believe,' he continued, smoothly ignoring her strangled outburst. 'While it's some time since I last dated anyone, I've no intention of breaking the vows I made yesterday.'

Something hard lodged in her stomach. He met her gaze steadily, yet that unspoken emotion swirled and still she couldn't decipher it.

'I'm sure I can cope,' he added.

Darcie, poor fool that she was, would have

told him he didn't have to 'cope' at all. He could have *her* as a lover here and now. But it turned out her supposedly philandering ex-boss had developed a chivalrous streak.

'What about you, Darcie?' He leaned back. 'How long since you last went on a date?'

She stared at him wordlessly. There was literally nothing she could say to that.

'You've an insight into my life, yet I've none into yours,' he added. 'You're quite the closed book.'

'Not at all. You know my life is spent working for you. All the hours.'

'Not the very small ones in the middle of the night,' he countered.

'It's not going to be a problem,' she mumbled.

'You're going to be able to cope?' His voice was light but there was an intensity she didn't understand in his gaze.

'Of course.' She wasn't going to miss something she'd never had.

Except she was starting to *crave* that very thing and it made her butterfingered and clumsy. She ached for his touch. She was thinking about it all the time, worse she was reading interest—*intimacy*—into details she knew he didn't even mean: his occasional hesitation, that teasing smile, the way he watched her...like the way he was watching her *now*.

His smile suddenly deepened, turning him even more impossibly handsome. And he knew it, didn't he? Darcie glared at him. Was he *provoking* her?

Well, maybe she'd do the last thing *he* expected of *her*. Maybe she'd confound him. Maybe she *would* spend his money today.

'It seems you're all over everything today,' she said. 'I'm going to go make my preparations for tonight,' she said huskily. 'I'll be sure to charge it to your account.'

And she was going to enjoy every second of it.

Elias showered and dressed in a fresh shirt and suit. The meetings had been interminable but successful and more pleasingly, he'd had significant success in his plans for their return to London. Darcie wanted to put forward the best application for Lily and he would ensure that happened.

Now all he had to do was get through the damned dinner party he'd agreed to celebrate with Vince and his wife. But Darcie hadn't been in the suite when he'd got back. For a moment he wondered if she'd left. But then the concierge had phoned to tell him she'd been slightly delayed.

She'd never been delayed before.

He walked to the window, not really seeing the city skyline at sunset. He'd barely slept—firstly he'd made all those arrangements, then his mind had been too busy replaying the day's events, incredulous at the decisions he'd made and the action he'd taken. Yet he didn't regret it. More astoundingly he'd scarcely been able to wait for her to wake to see how she'd handle him today.

'I'm sorry I'm late,' she called from behind him. 'I didn't appreciate how long a full beauty treatment takes.'

'Was it your first?' He turned to face her.

'Actually, yes, it was.'

But Elias couldn't reply. Couldn't tease any more. Couldn't think.

'Did the meeting go well?' she asked.

'Hmm?'

'With Vince.'

Oh. 'Yeah.'

'Elias?'

He just stared.

She walked forward and waved her hand in front of his face. 'Are you okay?'

'Yes.' He blinked, but it didn't matter. He was still transfixed.

'Really?' A caustic note sounded in her voice even as the colour in her cheeks steadily deepened. 'You're going speechless on me? Just because of a dress?'

It wasn't the dress. Although that was a stunning silky confection that enhanced her height and shape. And he'd never seen her with her hair loose either; she always had it tied back—either in a ponytail or a plait, or coiled into a bun. Tonight it wasn't pinned back at all. It was longer than he'd realised and it shone in the light and he wanted to run his fingers through it. But it wasn't her hair rendering him brainless, either. It was the shimmer in her eyes and the sparkle in her teasing smile, and they were not created by cosmetics. That was spirit. Vitality. Darcie herself. All Darcie. The part of Darcie she'd kept hidden from him for such a long time.

'Uh…' He cleared his throat. 'You're glowing.'

'Oh. That must have been the full body massage.' She suddenly smiled. 'I've never had one of those before, either.'

'Haven't you?' He almost choked as he blinked away the images that sprang to mind. 'And you're usually in grey.'

Until yesterday he'd only ever seen her in those trouser suits. With minimal make-up, it had been a simple, perfectly acceptable style that she'd never switched up despite the steady increases to her pay packets. But now that silky blue wrap-style dress showed skin. Smooth, satiny skin that screamed warmth and softness. He'd known those curves were there—the usual uniform of loose blouses and wide-legged pants couldn't hide everything. They'd hinted, tantalised. And maybe because he'd not looked for so long, now he couldn't stop staring.

'Yes. It was my intention to be as unobtrusive as possible.'

Unobtrusive? He stared at her for another second before an involuntary laugh shook him. She looked shocked, then insecure. Instant regret swamped him. Darcie was *vulnerable*. And he'd been such a fool to ever think she were as emotionless as he.

'The grey accentuates your eyes. They're the palest blue...' But now this dress brought out a different shade. It brought warmth. He stepped forward and took her hand. 'You could never, *ever* be unobtrusive, Darcie.'

For a second she looked stricken again. And he understood she'd *wanted* to be. She'd wanted to hide. She'd never wanted to draw attention to herself.

'Why would you want to be?' Why, when she was so beautiful, so capable, so fierce? Because she was fierce now.

'Unobtrusive is safe.' She bit her lip but kept her head lifted. That blue of her eyes was now the narrowest of rings around pupils that were dark and dilated and drew him closer still.

'Safe?'

'If you're not seen, you're less likely to be sent away. Old habits, I guess.' She lifted her chin. 'Is this okay or should I change?'

Okay? The silk hugged some curves, skimmed others, and the tips of his fingers screamed with the desire to slide the material away altogether.

'What do you want to do?' he asked huskily.

Heat surged. Not just the stirrings of attraction that he ought to suppress. This was a tsunami.

'We should go,' Darcie breathed. 'They'll be waiting.'

Yet neither of them moved.

Elias didn't give a damn about the deal anymore. He wanted to pull her close and explore every one of those generous curves. She was a voluptuous, sensual goddess and he wanted to stay right here and learn so many more of her secrets.

'Elias.' She swallowed. 'This is what you wanted.'

Two hours later and Elias couldn't recall a single reason why he'd ever wanted to attend this celebratory dinner. Watching Darcie attempt to

tackle a full four courses was a sensorial nightmare. He wasn't surprised at all to see her skip
dessert in favour of a cheese selection.

He'd tried to keep the conversation on business as much as possible. Tried not to stare at
Darcie too much. But, given she was seated
opposite him, it had been impossible. He was
ready to abandon the attempt altogether.

'You're very patient to put up with business
meetings only the day after your wedding.'
Vince Williams smiled at Darcie.

'To be honest I understand more about hedge
funds than I do about being a bride,' said Darcie.

'You've plenty of time to figure the marriage
bit out.' Cora lifted her glass. 'Are your parents
excited?'

Elias braced, realising too late he'd not considered the fact they might impose into Darcie's past. But she answered before he could
divert them.

'I don't have much family,' she said. 'I grew
up in the foster system.'

'Oh.' Vince instinctively leaned forward.
'That can be very challenging. Years ago Cora
and I fostered a number of young people.'

'Oh?' Darcie was noncommittal.

Elias got the sense not all foster experiences
were equal. Not in Darcie's world.

'Teens mostly,' Cora added. 'The ones who

were considered too old for long-term placement but who didn't thrive in group homes. We tried to offer them a couple of years of stability and offer some skills.'

Darcie carefully sliced a piece of cheese but didn't eat it. 'Are you still in contact with any?'

'Some. Not all.'

'A lot had had it rough,' Cora elaborated on Vince's answer. 'They'd been isolated a long time.'

'Yes.' Darcie smiled. 'I was lucky to find some close friends in the system. We made our own family.'

She meant Zara. Maybe even that guy Shaun. Lonely kids banding together, trying to forge themselves a better future. He hadn't any real idea about her past before now. At work she was more than businesslike, she was reticent. A fact he'd appreciated on an unconscious, instinctive level. Because knowing more about Darcie would have been intriguing—fascinating in fact. But now she wasn't his assistant, she was his wife, and he *ought* to know everything because he ought to be able to ease the edge of distress he knew she was near. But he couldn't.

'And now you have Elias.'

Darcie nodded.

'Perhaps you'll be able to build a bigger family together.'

'Perhaps,' Darcie murmured. 'If we're lucky.'

He couldn't take his gaze off her then, seeing that yearning so close to the surface. Apparently his self-control over his own mind was obliterated. All he wanted was to cart her upstairs and discover for himself every tiny detail.

He lifted the water glass and knocked back a deep sip. Having to battle rampant sexual thoughts in the middle of a business dinner was unacceptable. But he kept replaying that pathetic kiss in his head. Why hadn't he taken advantage of that opportunity? Why hadn't he pulled her close and explored the chemistry he knew they had? The electricity from the simplest, tamest of touches had him on edge. His warning system sent chills down his spine. Their situation was volatile, their new status wasn't stable, this could blow up in his face. Yet he couldn't resist leaning nearer.

Because now, as the conversation moved on, Darcie relaxed—she even laughed. And Elias discovered that relaxed, laughing Darcie was pure torture. The change within—the inability to put these thoughts out of his head?

'You're even cleverer than I thought, Elias,' Vince said shrewdly. 'Your sublime assistant is now yours forever.'

'Sublime assistant?' Darcie overheard the words and echoed them, a full octave higher.

Vince smiled at her. 'That's how he referred to you more than once.'

Darcie turned to Elias with a stunned expression. *'Sublime?'*

Vince and Cora both laughed. But Elias saw how genuine her shock was. And then the flash of hurt she fast hid. Did she really not know?

'It's true.' Elias desperately reached for the water glass again and pretended to direct his comment to Vince. 'I wanted Darcie from the first moment I saw her.' He watched the sweep of colour surge beneath her skin and she looked to the table. 'But she worked for me.'

So he couldn't touch. He'd told her that, hadn't he? But hadn't she believed him?

'You're not working for Elias now, Darcie?' Cora asked.

'No,' Darcie said. 'I'm taking a little time off and then I'll find something different.'

'I'd offer you a job anytime, Darcie,' Vince said.

A flare of anger smoked the last of Elias's brain cells. Fortunately Darcie spoke before he could.

'I'm not in the market for a new job right now, but in the future if that changes, I might call.'

Elias ground his teeth. That wouldn't be changing in the future. He'd keep her occupied.

With something. Anything. Maybe something very basic—such as himself.

He'd seen little of the passionate, emotional side of Darcie prior to yesterday. And the more he saw of it, the more he wanted, the *nearer* he wanted. He wanted her to talk to him. To tell him. To ask him again. But she was too good at masking her emotions. In the office he'd relied on that ability to keep her head cool. And her ability to keep up to his speed. She'd often explained things to others that second or third time that he didn't have the time or patience for. He only needed tell her something once and she had it locked in.

Now he realised what he'd done. And what he'd not done.

He'd told her *no*, once. He'd not kissed her properly at their wedding. He'd left her alone on what was their wedding night.

So what had she learned from him doing—and not doing—all that? Did she really think him seeing her as sublime was *shocking*?

He needed to get behind the wall she was trying to rebuild. He wanted more of challenging, confrontational, bold and brave Darcie. The one who spontaneously laughed and who not-so-secretly adored soft French cheeses. Who'd once invited him to—

'Where are you going on your honeymoon?'

Cora looked at them from one to the other in the following pause that neither of them filled. 'You are going on a honeymoon?'

Elias was too focused on Darcie to answer. Her pillowy lips had just parted in surprise. He'd tasted and she'd softened—far too briefly. Now he wanted her to soften against him again. Now he wanted to pull her into his lap and kiss her until she was hot and sighing and asking him to take her to bed.

'Eventually,' Darcie smoothed over the moment as Elias entirely failed to answer. 'We're just finalising some work first.'

'All work and no play isn't healthy for anyone, and certainly not a newly married couple.' He didn't know if it was Vince or Cora who answered her.

'We're aligned in our desires.' Huskiness entered Darcie's voice.

Elias couldn't resist playing up to the frisson she'd lit—even it was unintentionally. 'We very much like the same things.'

It was true.

'A power couple.' Vince chuckled. 'There's certainly an energy between you.' He leaned back at winked at Darcie. 'But I do wonder which of you is really the boss?'

No one was the boss of Darcie.

'We take turns,' she deflected lightly.

He was unbearably aroused by the ideas that innocuous statement set off in his head. All he wanted to do was to have her aloof focus fully, exclusively on him. He wanted bold Darcie of two weeks ago back. The one who hadn't hid her desire. Who couldn't. Because now *he* couldn't.

'You look like someone who's found long-lost buried treasure and can't actually believe it,' Vince said to him quietly when Cora and Darcie were engaged in conversation.

Yeah, and he wasn't about to let some raider come and steal it. She was his. She always had been. He'd just been blind to the fact. But he'd woken up now. 'You won't mind if we wrap this up?'

Vince laughed. 'Not at all.'

He never skimped on time with clients and certainly not prospective acquisitions. But he didn't care about business tonight. Tonight he needed to be with Darcie. Properly. He less than smoothly said goodbye on behalf of them both and Vince and Cora, bless them, headed off. Which left him alone with her at last.

Just before pushing the button to summon the lift, he turned to her and made his play. 'Come upstairs with me?'

CHAPTER EIGHT

DARCIE DESPERATELY NEEDED to get out of the lift. He'd echoed that mortifying invitation she'd made to him. But he'd meant it as merely a teasing reference and it was only infuriating because she was too frustrated to see the funny side.

'It was a very successful evening.' He followed up as the doors finally slid open.

'Do you think?' Darcie ground her teeth as she walked into the glittering lounge of the hotel's penthouse suite. They were finally alone and she could get away from him. Sitting opposite a tuxedoed Elias Greyson had stolen one appetite while stoking another and it had been almost impossible to concentrate on even the lightest of social conversation.

Tomorrow they would return to London. Not soon enough. They'd get on with the application for Lily. Everything was going to plan yet she felt unbearably edgy. Jumpy. Yeah, *frustrated.*

'I didn't know about their involvement with foster children,' she said, trying to divert her thoughts. That hadn't just startled her, it had raised her suspicions.

'Nor did I.' He followed her progress into the

lounge, his intensity building when she shot him a sceptical look. 'You don't believe me?'

'It's just a little convenient that you take your former foster child bride to meet the man you want to impress and it turns out *he's* been a foster parent.'

'I didn't know you were ever in the foster system till yesterday, Darcie, and I'd already offered to marry you by then.'

She knew her angry reaction was illogical, but she was still cross with him.

'Besides which—' he rubbed his jaw thoughtfully '—I had no real need to impress him.'

She turned jerkily. 'I know. But it makes me nervous to see how easily you can lie.'

'I can lie?' he echoed idly, and smoothly slipped his jacket off. 'When did I lie?'

'Tonight. With Vince.'

'Oh.' He tossed his jacket onto the nearby armchair and slowly advanced on her. 'What do you think I lied about?' He untied his tie and undid the top button of his shirt.

'When you said…' She was distracted by his slow undressing and increasingly awkward that she'd said anything at all. She should have made like him last night and gone straight to her bedroom.

'I didn't lie to Vince, Darcie. I never lie,' he

said softly. 'For the record, every word I spoke tonight was true.'

No, it wasn't. She instinctively took a step backwards.

His mouth quirked. 'Can you explain which bit bothered you?'

Well, she wasn't about to repeat it now.

'Don't hold back, Darcie.' His voice dropped to a whisper. 'I want to know what you're really thinking. I know you've not always felt in a position to do that before. But now is different, isn't it?'

It was appalling the way she melted when he said that. She swallowed.

'I never thought you'd be a coward,' he jeered lightly as he kept walking towards her with the feline grace of some dancer. Or predator. 'But I thought we pulled off the image of happy newlyweds without needing to lie at all.'

That assessment annoyed her even more. She didn't want to be beholden to him. 'The whole thing is stupid,' she muttered as she kept backing away from him. 'I shouldn't have had to do all this.'

She wanted to be there for Lily. She knew she could take care of Lily without needing—

She hit the wall. Literally. She huffed and put her hands on her hips and glared at him. 'The last thing I wanted to do was actually get married to anyone. *Ever.*'

'No?' His eyes widened but he still kept walking. 'Ditto. Yet inexplicably, here we are.'

He stopped, right in front of her. For a charged moment she glared up at him only then, to her shock, Elias smiled at her. And she suddenly giggled. A pop of laughter just bubbled up and burst out.

'You never wanted to marry?' He asked when she sobered—almost instantly. 'Not ever?'

'Of course not,' she mumbled. 'I know I can take care of Lily all by myself. I don't need some guy rescuing us. But they just won't accept that I'm good enough on my own.'

'Good enough?' He regarded her solemnly. 'Darcie—'

'Don't. I know it's not true.' She had to believe that. It was why she was fighting to do everything she could. 'But it's the way of the world, right?'

'Maybe.' A glimmer of a tease resurfaced. 'What of love, Darcie? Don't you believe in that either?'

Her heart puckered. She held little hope that *she* would ever find it. 'Truthfully I haven't seen many examples of long-term happily married couples.' She swallowed. 'Except maybe Cora and Vince.'

'Yeah, they seem pretty together,' Elias murmured. 'Are you going to tell me what it is you think I lied to him about?'

He was too near now. Too near, too big, too stunning. She couldn't say anything.

'Darcie...' He gazed down at her and his voice roughened. 'Ask me again.'

She knew he wasn't talking about tonight any more.

He leaned closer. 'That night you asked me to come upstairs with you, you meant to come to bed.'

Yes. His nearness sent her brain into meltdown. She was so tempted to breathe the truth. Too tempted. And it paralysed her.

'What if I promised the answer would be different this time?' He gently brushed her hair back from her flushed face. 'Where has my confident, capable, calm Darcie gone?'

My Darcie?

She closed her eyes. 'Confident, capable calm Darcie was all a fake.'

'No. I don't believe that,' he countered. 'Not for all that time.'

Not for work maybe. But when it came to this—to intimacy—there was no confidence, no capability and certainly no calm. She couldn't hold back the raw reality any more. 'You want the truth, Elias?'

'*Yes.*' A heartfelt whisper she couldn't ignore. 'Always.'

She opened her eyes and stared straight into his. 'I've never slept with anyone.'

He stilled. She saw him mentally repeating her statement. Saw the widening of his eyes as her words registered and felt the withdrawal of the warmth.

'*That's* what I was asking from you,' she added before he could say anything that would only mortify her more. 'It's *why* I asked you that night. Because I thought I was getting married and even though it wasn't going to be real...' She shrugged her shoulders. 'I wouldn't have the chance again, not for...'

'Because you'd be loyal even though it was going to be a paper marriage.'

'Yes,' she admitted softly. 'So I wanted...'

'Something for yourself first.' He gazed down into her eyes. 'Your first. Me. For one night.'

'Right.'

Elias couldn't breathe as the oddest sensations unfolded within him. Anger. Hunger. Protectiveness. Possessiveness. All at the same time. He was unravelling and the terrible, terrible urge to take her was taking precedence.

But he froze. Because discovering this now meant that this marriage—this supposed elegant solution to her problem—was suddenly a whole problem within itself. He'd thought they'd overcome their former status as employer and employee. He'd thought she was now his *equal*. But she wasn't. She was inexperienced not just with men, but in other relationships. too. She hadn't had a family. She'd felt so vulnerable it was her default status to try to stay beneath the radar in her suits.

And he *had* to walk away. He couldn't take the responsibility of doing this. 'You must be tired. It's been an intense thirty-six hours.'

Her eyes widened. 'Tired?'

He didn't sleep with virgins. He had flings with women as worldly as he was. Women who enjoyed the expensive restaurants to which he took them. Who enjoyed the jet and nice jewels and who didn't expect anything much more than great food and even better sex. An evening's pleasure was very straightforward and very finite and there was no emotional burden.

He rubbed his chest, surprised by the sudden ache there. Darcie was effectively bound to him, but she was more forbidden than ever. When he'd spent the evening—hell, many other evenings, too, if he were being honest—fantasising about taking her to bed and imagining her response. But knowing now that it would be her first time? Logically it shouldn't matter, yet it did. He remembered her unexpected behaviour that night in Edinburgh. She'd had to *drink* to gain courage to ask him something other women offered all the time with a literal bat of their eyelids.

Yeah, while Darcie was worldly and was wise in so many other ways, he also now knew she'd experienced things no one should have to endure—abandonment, isolation, fear for her security. And in this she was unbelievably inexperienced. In relationships.

And honestly, so was he. He didn't do them. He didn't do emotional support. He was rubbish at it. He'd inherited the lack from *both* parents. He'd failed his mother and he wasn't letting anyone else down ever. So he couldn't take her on in this. Because she'd need more than just *sex*, wouldn't she? And she should have it. She should have much more than the little he could ever offer.

'It really makes that much difference?' Reproach bruised the blue of her eyes.

Oh, she was pissed off with him. And it made everything ten times worse.

'Yeah. It does.'

'Because now you think I'm somehow deficient? Or incompetent in my decision-making?'

'No.' His frustration swirled. 'I just... I don't want you to feel obligated towards me.'

Because he'd married her, to help her. And everything was all muddied in his head.

'And *I* don't want you to feel any kind of obligation towards me, either. I don't want your *pity* kisses, Elias, just because you now know I'm inexperienced. I knew I shouldn't have told you. Do you really think I can't separate feelings of gratitude from lust?'

'So you do feel gratitude.' That was the last thing he wanted.

'*And* lust. Or does the latter not count?' She tilted her chin at him. 'Do you really think I'm attracted to you because I see you as some kind of rescuer to me? Do you think my feelings aren't fully formed?'

He stared at her. 'Feelings?'

'I have a number towards you right now, Elias. Anger being one. And yes, lust is another. You don't seem to mind other women wanting you. Is it just me who's not allowed to appreciate your form because I've never done this before?'

'My form?'

'You're physically compelling, yes. You always have been.'

'You have a lot going on,' he said stubbornly.

'Most people do,' she said. 'Even you. But you bury it deep and use work to block it off. And maybe, when there's a lot going on, there's something to be said for a blow-out. You do that. Just not with me. That's fine. You don't have to. So you can stop making excuses because I'm beyond embarrassed, I don't care anymore. You don't have to want me. But you didn't need to lie about it tonight.'

He gritted his teeth. 'I *didn't* lie.' He stepped forward, right into her space. 'Darcie—'

'Don't come near me now,' she snapped. She was so angry with him.

But he didn't back off. He stayed still.

He was the only man she'd *ever* considered asking. And he was only one she'd thought might actually agree. She knew he liked sex. She'd seen him date an array of women over the time she'd worked for him. So she'd thought that maybe…maybe he'd have said yes to one night even as a novelty or something. Because she'd also known—courtesy of the hours they spent working—that he'd not dated a woman in a while *recently*. She'd half hoped he'd have been feeling base-level sexual frustration that he'd have been happy to act on. But he hadn't. He'd rejected her. Immediately. Coolly. And he'd done it again now. She should have known he was always going to deny her. Everyone did. So she was going to remain a virgin wife. Unclaimed. Unwanted. She was always unwanted. As a child she'd sought a family for so long and never got one. Even now as an adult she didn't get the things other people got. And she was furious about it.

'You're upset.' Elias remained like a statue.

'Yes. So I might say something I regret. I might—' She broke off and blinked back angry tears. 'Just leave me alone, Elias.'

'I'm not leaving you while you're upset.'

'Even if your presence makes me all the more upset?'

His hands fisted by his side. 'I've tried do what you want, Darcie.'

'What I want?'

Not everything. Not *nearly* everything. But she was selfish and impetuous and greedy, and it hadn't worked, and she wasn't going to ask anymore. She wasn't going to risk rejection all over again. It hurt too badly because she wanted it too much.

'You look at me with those big blue eyes. Did you know they shimmer, Darcie?' He growled. 'And there are secrets in there. Tell me your secrets.'

'I just did.' Her voice croaked. 'And still you said no.'

'Because hedonism doesn't seem like your style, Darcie. You're more serious than that.'

'Well, I've never really had the chance to find

out, have I? There've always been other considerations.'

'Aren't there other considerations still?'

'They're not going to change.' She waved an irritated hand. 'Our sleeping together wouldn't have changed anything, either. It was one night.'

'Naive Darcie. It would change things. And one night would never be enough.' He dragged in a breath. 'Did you ask anyone else after I turned you down?'

'Obviously not.' She was so shocked by the question she snapped the answer instantly.

'Because you'd thought about me.' His voice was low and that husky edge signalled danger. 'Because you only wanted *me*.'

'Really, Elias?' Her rebellion flared. 'You want a complete ego trip?'

'We have chemistry, Darcie, and chemistry is something I can do. But this marriage isn't forever. *That's* not going to change. So if we sleep together, even though it's going to be good, it won't change the fundamentals. It won't change our future.'

'Do you think I *want* it to?' She was even more furious with him. 'You really are arrogant. I just told you I never *wanted* to get married and I certainly don't want to stay that way!'

'Good.' He stepped in closer still. 'Then ask me to kiss you.'

'*What?*'

Oh, he really wanted the full ego trip. But he was so close now. So hot he was crowding her with his scent and his intensity, and her thinking ability was sliding.

'Ask me.'

Her heart pounded in her ears and that heat had exploded, scorching her from the inside out.

'I won't do it until you ask me again.' His breath brushed hers. His lips were so close. And she was so confused.

'You want me to ask you for…?' Her furious drawl was a bare mumble. 'A kiss?'

'Good enough.' His lips covered hers.

The brush of his mouth was gentle, too gentle. It made her ache worse and she gasped, a breathy moan.

He lifted fractionally away. 'Ask me again.'

That deep ache overcame her anger. She wanted more. 'Kiss—'

He did. Stronger than before, yet impossibly even more tender. Her heart pounded as he slid his fingers through her hair. He tilted her head so he could deepen the kiss and she arched closer to meet him. His tongue lashed hers, giving her a desperately needed taste of deeper intimacy. But when he pulled away again her brain kicked back online.

'Ask—'

'What are you doing?' she interrupted reproachfully.

'Training you,' he said softly.

'*Training* me?' She glared into his face. 'Like some performing animal?'

His pupils were so blown she couldn't see the blue for the black.

'I want you to understand that when you ask me for something, I'll deliver.' The intensity of his answer literally shook her.

But she was lost to emotional intensity, too, and her most deep-seated yearning was torn out.

'What if I don't want to have to always *ask* for everything?' She growled. 'Why can't I just be gifted it? Why do *I* always have to fight so hard to get a few things that others seem to get so easily?'

Fiercely devastated, she shoved him away. Hard.

But he didn't move and she was suddenly *so* exposed. She lifted her hands to hide but he grabbed her wrists and pulled them to her sides. She closed her eyes so she wouldn't have to see his pity. So he couldn't see the stupid yearning in her.

'Darcie,' he muttered. '*Darcie.*'

'*Don't* pity me.'

His grip on her wrists tightened and he suddenly leaned in, pressing the full weight of his body against her. Pinning her to the wall with every inch of him.

'Feel me,' he muttered. '*Feel* me, Darcie.'

She did. She felt the coiled steel of tense muscles and the rapid thud of his heart. She felt the swerving emotions—frustration, anger, *arousal*. It was there—his huge, hard shaft pressing deep against her belly. She quivered uncontrollably and he pushed closer still. Her breath hitched, shortening as sensation—yearning—tumbled inside.

'*This* is how I've wanted you,' he growled. 'Here like this. With me. So close that...' He dragged in a difficult breath. 'From the moment we met. But from that moment you were my employee.'

Her throat was so dry she couldn't swallow. She couldn't move—and yet she was, secretly her insides were shifting. Her blood was heating, muscles softening—priming. Not just her insides. Goosebumps lifted on her skin as she shivered and her breasts tightened—her nipples peaking, pushing back against him. Welcoming him.

For a long moment they remained sealed together. So still. But their breathing shifted—hot and shallow, faster and faster as desire surged to the point of detonation.

'My father had an affair with his secretary,'

he said harshly. 'It was a mess. For her. For my mother. For my whole family.' His tension built and stiffened his muscles, and he instinctively tightened his grip on her wrists. 'So you'll understand it was a line I could never, *ever* cross.'

She also understood that it had cost him something to tell her that.

'But you're not my employee now.' His mouth was by her ear. A hot, husky, *hungry* whisper.

She couldn't see his eyes but she could breathe in his scent, his heat, his intensity, and she understood she was about to get everything he could share of himself. Everything she wanted.

'I want to kiss you again, Darcie. And if I do, I won't want to stop. Is that okay with you?'

She felt him, believed him, and all the need she'd locked away for so long surged. 'Yes.'

CHAPTER NINE

SHE DIDN'T KNOW what she'd expected but for some reason his total tenderness was a shock. The kisses he dropped on her cheek and jaw and then her neck were soft and light, and he was so unbearably careful her eyes stung. She closed them and released her caught breath on a sigh of blurred delight and despair. She wanted this. Him. *So much.* His thumbs swirled over the fragile skin on the inside of her wrists and the simple caresses swept her further and faster along the tide of arousal—of *emotion.* Thank goodness for the wall at her back; she was literally melting. He crowded closer, sensing she needed support, and slid his leg between hers. It only made her heat and soften even more. 'Elias…'

'I'm not going anywhere.' A husky promise that made her quiver.

His grip on her wrists tightened and he lifted them, placing her hands on his shoulders. Finally she was free to cling and she did. Shamelessly.

'Please.' She *needed* his kiss.

He lifted his head and gazed into her eyes as he glided his hands back down her arms, torching skin that was already ablaze for him before dropping them to her waist. He nudged his leg closer and tightened his hold on her. She couldn't resist rocking her hips ever so slightly as the hard heat of him pressed right where she ached most and she heard the answering hitch in his breathing. His eyes gleamed as he leaned in.

'Darcie.'

Her response was effervescent and uncontrollable. She met him, her tongue swirling—dancing—with his. She needed the kisses deeper, to be everywhere. She needed him like this—his whole body flush hot and hard against hers—and she needed to touch *him* everywhere. Yet her fingers could only curl into his shoulders and cling. Desperate, she shook—unable to stand any more. But Elias had her. With an exultant growl he scooped her into his arms, effortlessly tossing her lightly to adjust his hold. Pressed close to his chest, she threaded her fingers through his hair as he carried her to the bedroom he'd taken last night. He smiled at her—a laughing, lustful smile the likes of which she'd never seen—as he placed her smack in the centre of the big bed.

Darcie then stared, slack-jawed, as he took charge. He'd never looked as handsome. Her innards liquefied as he pulled something from his pocket and tossed it up so it landed near the pillow. She glanced, realised it was protection. And he'd had it on him already? He'd considered this might happen? Her heart raced as she turned back to watch him toe off his shoes while also unbuttoning his shirt. Two seconds later he'd shucked his trousers in record time. She sank deeper into the mattress as he advanced on her clad only in black boxers.

'You're far too well-dressed for this,' he muttered.

He toyed with the slippery satin fabric of her dress, seeking the hidden fastenings, the zip, and releasing them with practiced ease. She shifted as he worked, helping him slide the material from her.

A pause, an intake of breath from them both as her skin was bared. Spread before him in only lacy bra and panties, Darcie couldn't believe this was happening. But the expression in his eyes grounded her in searing reality. The intensity, the concentration, the evident desire in his body all combined to set her every sense alight. But this wasn't only superficially hot. This burned on the inside, too. With every kiss, every caress, he heated her *heart*—melting it, re-forming it, making it his.

'Elias…' she gasped.

She was completely naked in moments. And he was kissing parts of her no other person had ever seen, let alone touched. Her breathing quickened even more and she stretched out her hands seeking purchase but finding only the soft silken sheets. Her fingers curled into fists as he touched her, teased her, *tasted* her. With every lush swirl of his tongue he showed her how searingly hot such an intimacy could be and just how responsive her own body was. And how much her body hungered for *his*. She strained upwards, locking her hips as he drove her swiftly towards the brink of ecstasy. One arm holding her in place, he growled, a guttural husk of approval, before deepening his attentions—sliding a skilled fingertip inside while sealing his mouth to her highly sensitive bud and repeatedly lashing her there with his tongue. Darcie screamed as the sensations tumbled, her body convulsing in pleasure as wave upon wave hit and he held her tighter still, helping her ride it through.

She breathed hard in recovery but even through the aftershocks, arousal resurged. Because his hand was still cupping her intimately, his finger locked inside her. But he'd moved higher up the bed so he could look into her eyes.

'Do you want the rest of me?' he asked bluntly, raggedly.

The ferocity of arousal in his expression made her breathless all over again. She couldn't yet speak. Couldn't yet comprehend the power of what she'd just experienced. And that there was more to come?

'Darcie?' Strain tightened his face.

He began to slide free of her but she clamped down, desperate to keep him deep inside her. His gaze bored into hers.

'I have many talents, but mind-reading isn't one of them, sweetheart,' he muttered roughly. 'I understand that you don't want to ask for everything all of the time, but you're still going to have to communicate with me on some things.'

'Like you do with me?' she challenged softly, feeling a foreign power flood through her now. Feeling confidence in her sensuality for the first time ever. Feeling as if she knew what she wanted and she knew how she might get it. 'It works both ways, Elias. And I don't know that either of us is too good at communicating when it comes to personal things.'

He took a couple of deep breaths of his own. As if he, too, were seeking recovery. And control. 'I wanted to hear you ask me again,' he admitted huskily. 'Last time I couldn't answer the way I wanted, and I wanted a do-over. I wanted to feel that burst of…'

She fell a little harder for him, burned a little hotter. 'Are you saying I made your day with my offer?'

'You made my decade.'

Arousal flooded her and she knew he knew. Because he felt it—the slickening of her channel. His eyes smouldered and she felt his muscles bunch.

'Yet you denied me.' Her reproach was husky.

'You know I had to. But I've thought about you for so long.'

She couldn't resist rocking harder into his hand, seeking more from the fingers that had resumed their soft, skilled torment. 'Elias—'

'I watched you when I thought it was safe. When you were focused on your screen or had your back to me, and I wondered if you ever looked at me when I wasn't looking at you, too.' He pressed closer, quickly kissing her nearest straining nipple as he then confessed, 'Like a teen with a crush. I wondered and wished and was so uncertain because you were always so aloof you didn't even deign to dine with me. And then one night you appeared, and you looked me directly in the eyes and asked me to come upstairs with you.'

She was shallowly panting now.

'Part of me wanted to shout in celebration but I had to say no. And then you didn't look at me at all. I've still not forgiven you for that, Darcie.'

'It's scary how well you hid it,' she breathed. 'You seemed so cold.'

'I was *controlled*. There's a difference.'

She never would have guessed. She'd read his reaction as emotionless and she'd thought she could read him well—after all, it had been almost three years in which she'd seen that poker face in boardrooms and high-level meetings. She knew displeasure. She knew precision. Attack. But that most primal of emotions—lust. *That* she'd not seen in him. He could mask up frighteningly well. Could he hide other emotions, too? Other real, deep feelings? That possibility was something she filed away. Yet she had seen more in these last couple of days. She'd seen anger. *Amusement*. She even thought she'd seen the flash of jealousy.

'I never want to initiate something you don't want. I always want to know you're on board with me. It matters. I'm a powerful person. People say yes to me even when they might not want to. I never want that cloudiness so I always clarify consent. I always ask.' His gaze skittered down her body, taking in the stiffness of her needy nipples, the sheen of her heated skin, the rhythmic rock of her hips as she met his teasing fingers.

'That's a good thing.' She swallowed and licked her lips. 'But I think…with this…maybe you don't have to always ask. Maybe you can trust that if you start something, I'll tell you if I don't want it at that time...'

'And now?'

'You know I want it all. All of you.'

He closed his eyes briefly. Then moved.

Darcie was bereft at the sudden loss of intimacy, of any contact. But he was fast, reaching for the foil package he'd tossed down by the pillow. Her body went lax as she watched him discard his boxers and she saw him naked before her for the first time. She swallowed, nerves rising, as he rolled the condom down his broad, engorged length. He glanced over and smiled as he read her face.

'Don't worry, I'll help you,' he promised.

She nodded. She was going to need it, because she had no idea how—

He straddled her and began again—kisses, deep, lush kisses that made her brain evaporate, leaving her able to do nothing but feel. And that worry ebbed as his hands swept over her, reheating skin that had barely cooled, pushing her to an even higher state of need. She parted her legs instinctively, the empty ache at her core driving her.

He muttered something indecipherable and dropped his body onto hers. The weight of him was heavenly, offering both security and challenge. Looking into her eyes, he slid his hand between them, stroking her nub till she twisted, then he teased her apart. He nipped her lips and slid his tongue into her mouth, possessing her there as he retook her intimate space with not one finger, but two this time, gently teasing so she grew more supple and pliant with every caress. She moaned, drowning in desire. She knew he was preparing her, but she was more than ready now.

'Please,' she begged on a breathless groan. 'Please.'

He nudged her legs a little farther apart and slipped his hand from her only to grip himself, guiding the tip of his length to her slick, heated space.

Darcie stilled. The pressure was intense as he slowly breached her entrance. She couldn't breathe, couldn't move. All senses burned. She went tight and soft, hot and shivery all at the same time and moaned helplessly in the power of it. With a guttural growl Elias thrust hard and took total possession of her body. She gasped, both shocked and sated in that very second. He was there. *Hers*. And the sharp, stabbing pain disappeared as quickly as it had hit.

'Okay?' A strained plea from Elias.

She panted as she nodded. He kissed her— long and sensuous and still with that generous tenderness and time. Finally he eased from her only to press back deeper. Then harder. Then again. And Darcie looped her arms around his strong, slick back and held on. Held him close.

'Elias…'

'More?'

'Yes.' Her eyes watered—not from pain, but from the pure pleasure and the deep, deep emotion of this moment. 'Yes. *Yes.*'

It was glorious. *So* glorious as he showed her—shifting their angle, alternating the pace, teasing her. *Pleasing* her. She was breathless in seconds, instinctively rising to meet him with her hips, with hands, mouth. With everything she had. Her nipples were so tight and she loved the rub of his chest against them. Pleasure shot along every nerve ending and as he choked and changed up his hold to clutch her even more tightly to him and she began to shake.

'That's it. Oh, Darcie—'

Her name was lost in his throaty growl of pleasure while she could only shudder as the ecstasy hurtled her into oblivion.

She didn't know how long it was until he moved. But she kept her eyes closed, not wanting to return to reality. She wanted to remain floating in this bliss. Only then she felt him walking two fingers up her belly. They moved slow but firm, gently bypassing her navel before reaching her sternum. She quivered, passion and energy trickling back. Those two finger-tips moved an inch or two higher. Her nipples tightened in anticipation.

'Do I go left or right?' A deep, murmuring tease.

The giggle just bubbled up. She opened her eyes, looking to see him on his side facing her, his head propped on one hand. He looked flushed and dishevelled and yet still impossibly debonair. And the gleam in his eyes was pure satisfaction.

'You must be pretty pleased with yourself,' she murmured. 'I didn't know it was like that. I didn't know...' What she'd been missing out on for so long. 'Is it always...'

'So wonderful?' he said gently. 'No. I've never had it that wonderful.'

'You don't have to say that. Don't ruin it by—'

'Telling the truth?' One eyebrow rose. 'The truth is you're gorgeous, Darcie. Just gorgeous. And honestly I can't stop wanting to touch you.'

He stole her breath. Her words. Her mouth was his...her whole body was his all over again.

'For the record, you can touch me anytime you like.' He shot her a smile a whole lot later.

'Anytime, anyhow?' She couldn't resist teasing.

'Basically.'

She laughed.

His smile widened. 'You're going to take advantage of that permission, aren't you?'

'Possibly.' She shrugged, as if not that bothered. In truth she was going to do that any chance she had.

'I'm so glad.' He pulled her to rest against his chest.

Warm, sleepy, yet still intrigued, she traced the parts of him accessible to her with light fingertips—sating her curiosity, savouring the freedom she now had to touch him all she wanted. She glanced up and caught him gazing at her with an odd expression.

'What?' She paused her explorations.

But he covered her hand with his and pressed it back on his skin, encouraging her to continue. 'I'm struggling to understand how it's possible you've never had a sexual relationship before now.'

'You know working for you has taken up almost every waking moment for the last three years,' she muttered.

'But before that? You're twenty-three, Darcie. Was there no first love in your late teens?'

'Not for me.' She wrinkled her nose, because this totally wasn't a topic she wanted to consider right now. But at the same time she appreciated his interest and she couldn't resist opening up to him a little more. 'I wasn't…' She shook her head awkwardly. 'Zara always had a boyfriend. She was stunning and confident. I was the nerdy sidekick, third-wheel best friend who wasn't good at any of that stuff.'

'Darcie, trust me,' he said. 'You're good at everything.'

'*No one* is good at everything,' she countered realistically. 'Not even you.'

'What? You wound me!' He chuckled and rolled, pinning her beneath him as he laughingly interrogated her. 'At what do I fail?'

For a moment she stared up at him, basically seduced into brainlessness again already. But then she thought of something.

His gaze narrowed and she felt him brace as she started to laugh. 'You're worse than I am at taking holidays.'

CHAPTER TEN

'HOLIDAYS?' ELIAS ECHOED, assuming a perplexed air. 'What are these "holidays" you speak of?'

She giggled again and he couldn't resist kissing her. But when he lifted his head and gazed down at her he realised she was right. He couldn't remember the last time he'd bothered to take a sustained break from work. But why would he? Work was energy and excitement. He liked moving from one project to the next without time to take a breath—it *was* breath to him. But Darcie thought that he was *worse* than she was, which meant she'd take a break if she *could*. He'd been so very blind when it came to her. And in so many ways.

'In all this time working for me you've not taken any time off,' he mused. 'I probably should have been sued by an employee's federation or something. I'm pretty sure it's been illegal.'

'It was a privately negotiated contract,' she said valiantly. 'I wanted to work.'

Wanted to or *had* to? Because there was a difference. And he didn't like thinking of her *having* to. Nor did he like her trying to make him feel better about it. 'Doesn't make it okay, though. When did you last have a holiday?'

She dropped her gaze. 'School holidays.'

Well, that was a while ago. And also not true. 'You worked all of them,' he said. 'From your mid-teens you took whatever job you could—fast-food outlets, then data entry. Once you got your first job you never had a break. I rechecked your agency CV on the flight to Vegas.'

Her gaze shot back to his. 'You did? Why?'

'Because I realised that despite working alongside you for almost three years, I barely know anything substantial about you.'

She swallowed. 'You could've just asked me.'

'And you'd answer properly?' He watched her with wry amusement, feeling an odd ache in his chest at the same time. 'You're reticent about anything personal.' And now he just wondered all the more about her background. He had the horrible feeling she'd been very lonely. 'That was understandable in our working relationship, but now we're married...'

Her blue eyes turned intense. 'Well, you don't exactly offer up much personal, either.'

True. 'Perhaps it's a "work on" for us both. Let's trade.' He leaned back. 'You go first. Tell me, have you ever really travelled?'

'Frequently.' She shot him an impish grin. 'I'm very used to your private jet and still appreciate it, every time. Thanks to you I've seen the Eiffel Tower, the Colosseum in Rome, even the Hollywood sign in LA.'

'Those were literally fly-bys and not for recreational purposes.' He fiddled with the edge of the sheet, wary about asking too much too soon and uncertain as to why he suddenly wanted to know so badly. 'You never went on holiday with your foster family?'

Her expression instantly shuttered. 'It wasn't something many of them could afford.'

How many foster families had she been placed with?

'But you *can* afford it, yet you don't go on holiday either.' She deflected the focus back to him.

And yes, she had him there. 'I take long weekends.'

'Not often.' She looked back up at him. 'And not recently.'

Also true, and it was because he usually only took a long weekend on the request of a lover and there hadn't been one those in a while. His exes liked yachts, clubs, glamorous events—easily achieved in the short time format. Brief flings that didn't go emotionally deep. But Elias's expansion plans had kept him busy recently, and every weekend for the last four months he'd been working alongside Darcie.

They were together once more, but this weekend could be very different.

'We could stay here an extra day,' he suggested huskily.

'Wow.' Dry amusement sparked in her eyes. 'A whole extra day?'

'Yeah.' He refused to let her soft snark slay him, because something was better than nothing. 'It's a good offer, Darcie.'

'You think?' Her eyebrows arched but she shook her head. 'No. We should get back to London and get the application under way.'

'My lawyers are already gathering advice and information to prep us both. And it's the weekend—we could stay until tomorrow night and still be back in time for that meeting first thing Monday morning.'

For a second, temptation turned her eyes smoky, then she blinked. 'I meet Lily on Sunday afternoons.'

Of course. He'd forgotten. As had she, and he knew she felt guilty for that small lapse. But she needn't. It was okay to have been distracted. He smiled at her reassuringly. 'Then we'll stay today and return to London early tomorrow so you're home in time to meet her face-to-face.'

Her expression softened but there was wariness still there. 'Are you sure?'

Was she worried about disappointing him? He

really didn't want that. 'Absolutely.' He wanted to please her and he'd take what he could get. 'We can laze by the hotel pool, eat luscious food, literally do nothing for the day.'

That sly amusement sprang back into her eyes. 'It's not within your capability to do *nothing*.'

'That's very true.' He grinned at her. 'I guess I'll have to entertain myself with *you*.'

Twenty-four hours later Elias strode through the airport distracted by the memory of his adorably dishevelled wife struggling to fasten her safety belt in time for landing back in London. He'd quite deliberately stunned her with his attentions as they'd flown over the Atlantic, feeding that edgy need within him. The need that was determinedly refusing to abate in any way. But now the sultry, flushed smile she'd rewarded him with was stuck in his mind and all he wanted was to do it all over again.

'I'll drop you to your visit with Lily and pick you up after,' he said absently. It would give him just enough time to ensure everything was as he'd requested and, yeah, he was a little wary of how she was going to react to what he'd done.

'You're driving? Where's Olly?'

'I thought we might deal with the rest of the world tomorrow.' He didn't want to have to share her yet. One more night of this sensual bliss and then reality would return.

Darcie struggled to rein in her excitement as she played with the building bricks Lily favoured. It was only an hour, but the first face-to-face visit they'd had in a while.

'I'll see you next week?' Lily asked.

Darcie nodded. 'Of course.'

She couldn't promise the little girl anything more even though she desperately wanted to. But she would never promise Lily something she couldn't come through with because she knew all too well how it felt to have those promises broken. Repeated disappointments slowly destroyed a person.

But now the precious hour was up and she found Elias double-parked outside the building. She couldn't hold back her smile as she walked to the car. The man had so much more to him than she'd imagined. He wasn't only a workaholic billionaire, he was a playful *tease*. The way he'd sparked stunned her. As for his physical skills…sensations still tumbled inside her from the way he'd toyed with her on the jet. Appallingly, there was apparently no end to the neediness that surely should be eased after a weekend in which they'd barely left that big bed…all she wanted was for him to kiss her again. Now.

He was watching her as she struggled to fasten her seatbelt. Amusement curved his mouth, and heat shone in his eyes. 'You okay?'

She nodded jerkily.

'It was a good visit?'

'Yep.' She stared out the window trying to find a better distraction for her inappropriate brain. Then she realised their direction. 'This isn't the way to your penthouse.' They were moving out from the central city, not towards it.

'I know.' His hands tightened on the steering wheel. 'We're going to our new home.'

'Our what?'

'Home.' He cleared his throat. 'I thought it would be better for our chances with Lily if we had a house that's secure and warm and has everything she could want.'

'I didn't know you had an actual house.'

'I didn't.' He pulled into a quiet street in London. He got out his phone and tapped something on the screen. The large gates of a big property at the end of the street opened automatically. He turned into the driveway and the gates smoothly closed behind them.

Darcie gazed at the beautiful brick building. It was big, private, in a sheltered quiet street in a leafy, wealthy suburb. 'So you're renting this, just for now?' She swivelled in her seat face him.

He shook his head. 'Bought it.'

'*How?*' She gaped. 'Even for you, that's a fast deal.'

His grin flashed. 'It's been a busy few days. Come on, let's go exploring.'

But for a second Darcie could only stare after him as she struggled to compute what he'd just said. Did that mean that while she'd spent the weekend out of her mind with bliss in his arms, he'd been organising a house purchase on the side? How had he managed to do that? Because he'd have supervised all this even from the distance, no way would he have delegated it completely. Slowly she followed him. It wasn't that she didn't appreciate it, she was just stunned that he'd thought of so much while that whole time she'd barely been able to think at *all*. Clearly he hadn't been as swept away as she. And *that* was a reality check.

She drew breath as she glimpsed more of the property. 'There's a lawn.'

'A place for her to play, yes.' He unlocked the door with a security code and stood aside for her to enter. 'I believe it's a little sparsely furnished, it's been empty, but we can work on that.'

Darcie couldn't believe her eyes. The house was *four* stories high, spacious, stunning and doubtlessly eye-wateringly expensive. She walked through the two living spaces into the gorgeous open-plan kitchen and family living area.

'It's not a stone's throw from a Michelin restaurant but I got them to deliver us a few meals,' Elias drawled softly.

But Darcie was too blown away to be able to answer. The living area opened out to that lawn—a private little park already complete with a small swing and slide set. There was even a luxurious yet cosy cinema room farther down the corridor. Darcie could so easily see herself curled up on that big plush sofa watching the latest cartoon musical movies with Lily. Or snuggled next to Elias late at night…only Elias didn't watch movies, did he?

'You don't like it?'

'*Like* it?' She shook her head at him. 'It's incredible, Elias.'

He was incredible. She was stunned that he'd thought of all this, done all this in those few days.

His eyes narrowed on her. 'You can redecorate anything, of course, I won't be offended. It wasn't as if I chose anything in here.'

'You hired an interior designer.'

He nodded. 'A team have been working round the clock since Thursday.'

'And they've done a fantastic job. It's beautiful, Elias.'

'There are a couple of rooms for home offices. And a gym. An indoor pool. But the bedrooms are up here.' He led the way. 'I thought maybe this could be Lily's room.'

And there was the giveaway—he must have done a virtual tour of the place, planned out what he'd wanted, considered *everything*. She stopped just inside the doorway and stared at the framed photograph on the wall. It was the one photograph she had of Zara and Lily.

'I took a photo of the one in your wallet and a studio did a digital touch-up.' He looked awkwardly at her. 'I hope you don't mind.'

'*Mind?*' She blinked rapidly. Because Lily remembering Zara meant everything to Darcie and that photo was a personal touch that *he'd* thought of. 'It's a really nice thing to do.' Yet her nerves rose. 'How many bedrooms are there?'

'Seven. Even more bathrooms.'

Darcie's mind whirred. There was more than room for Lily. There was room for a whole *bunch* of kids. And was her lower belly aching all of a sudden? She pressed a hand to her stomach as for the first time in her life she realised she craved a child. She yearned to give Lily a sister. A brother, too. She would love to centre Lily in a huge, whole family. And *she* longed to be part of a huge, whole family, too. Something lurched inside as for the first time such a prospect didn't seem quite so impossible. But this was such a secret dream—something she'd always longed for but never let herself acknowledge…because it *was* impossible. Wasn't it?

'This is the main bedroom.' Elias had moved up to the next level.

Darcie stood in the doorway and absorbed the stunning room. There were wide windows opening onto a balcony with a view of the trees. There was a the massive bed made up with luxurious-looking linen. On the other side of the room an open door revealed a large dressing room. A selection of his clothes already hung there and the glimpse of the bathroom made her bones melt. She knew they'd both fit in that massive bath easily.

'I'll send someone to get your clothes from your flat,' he muttered.

Darcie's heart thudded. On one level this was so very real. They were going to live together and share that big bed and all of this most gorgeous *home*. The thought literally shook her. She had to turn her back. She had to walk away. She couldn't look at him just this second because she couldn't let him see how much this meant to her. He wouldn't have intended for her to take this as seriously, or as emotionally, as she was. This was nothing to him. He'd whipped up in a couple of days. But for her? This was like having her most secret wish granted.

A beautiful big home in which she'd live with the ones she loved.

It was everything she'd ever wanted. But it wasn't *real*—the intention was for *Lily*. Not for her. She had to remember that she and Elias weren't going to last. There weren't going to be siblings for Lily and there would be no forever for them. This was just for now. One year. Maximum. That was the deal.

Darcie was so silent Elias grew increasingly concerned. He followed her back downstairs to the living areas. 'I should have checked with you first.'

He'd stupidly thought it would be a good surprise but maybe she didn't like this part of London. Or the size of the house. Or the fact that she'd had no say in any of this whatsoever. He should have *asked* her. Should have given her choices.

Was it that big main bedroom that had freaked her out? Did she not want to sleep with him in there? But he'd deliberately chosen a large house so there would be plenty of room for them to have their own space. She could have her own bedroom if she preferred. Because they'd not discussed the duration of their affair at all. Perhaps she wanted it to end now they were back in Britain? He didn't know. And he hated not knowing. Hated thinking he'd somehow screwed up.

And still she didn't say anything.

Elias gritted his teeth. Turned out he *was* like his father—controlling everything, assuming that he knew everything and doing what he thought best without consultation. He felt increasingly awful. Chilled, he strove to regain his self-control. He couldn't let his emotion get the better of him here. He had to apologise. 'I should have—'

'Can we see the pool?'

He turned towards her. Darcie's eyes were shadowed but her cheeks were a little flushed. 'Of course.'

He followed her. The indoor pool was large and benefitted from clever lighting, calming decor. He watched Darcie walk the length of it. She opened the sleek cupboard at the end and stilled.

'There's everything in here.' She showed him a selection of child-sized inflatables stowed inside. 'You thought of everything.'

Her gratitude was too much and too unwarranted because really that had been the interiors team, not him. He'd only told them to prep it for a five-year-old's entertainment. And he'd not asked Darcie's opinion at all. 'You know you've not married a hero, right?' he said huskily. 'You've married a hunter.'

'That's what you think you are?' She actually giggled.

'You don't?'

For a moment their eyes met and he checked, reading her need. Anticipation rippled through him—blasting out the chill he'd felt before. Rendering him beyond control again.

'How deep is the water?' She suddenly seemed oddly breathless.

'I'm not sure,' he muttered. 'Did you want to find out?'

A smile flashed. Spontaneity sparked. He watched, utterly in thrall as Darcie unleashed and her vibrancy bubbled free. Her skin glowed and her blue eyes sparkled and her soft laughter bounced against the marble walls. He couldn't speak. It wasn't just the rush of sexual attraction but another sort underpinning him. It was new and solid and he wanted to hold on to the sensation. *Joy*, he realised. Unfettered, holistic joy. Because Darcie, now clad in just her underwear, dived into the water and stretched out like a gorgeous nymph.

'Zara loved the water,' she said. 'She'd jump in fountains on a hot day like this.'

Elias stood at the edge of the pool, unable to tear his gaze from her. 'She was a free spirit?'

'Absolutely.'

The lights beneath the water illuminated Darcie's face, making her glow even more brightly and as far as Elias was concerned, Darcie was the sprite. The nymph. The goddess.

'We'd escape to the park any time we could. Any park, but preferably one with a decent pond. Zara adored water lilies. Which is why Lily is named Lily, of course. She was such a romantic. Lily's a water baby, too.' Darcie floated on her back and smiled up at him. 'She's going to love this.'

Yeah? Elias was loving this, too. Because it was Darcie he was learning about and she was more free-spirited than he'd ever realised. More than she'd allowed him to see before now. Her circumstances had limited her ability to do as she desired. But now she was literally in a space in which she could do as she pleased. At least, he hoped she felt that way. Right now she seemed to and he wanted her to stay like this—purely, unashamedly her vibrant, sensual, playful self.

Sharing wasn't something he had much experience with. His dates had been more transactional—he provided entertainment, interesting destinations, a diamond bracelet or earrings to sparkle at the restaurant and to remember the night by. Very simple and straightforward. But this was different. Pool toys meant more and Darcie's obvious delight in all this was the best reward he could ever ask for.

Oh, who was he kidding? He wanted so much more. And now. He toed off his shoes and shrugged out of his shirt, glancing up to see Darcie treading water in the middle of the pool, watching him, with a different, smaller smile on her face. One that snared him completely. *Yes.*

Darcie was more siren than mermaid and right now she was summoning him to his fate. All he could do was dive in and surrender—to drown in her embrace.

CHAPTER ELEVEN

'THERE ARE SO many forms.'

Darcie spread paperwork across the table, baulking at the level of detail required. Elias's lawyers had visited first thing and they'd been full of confidence and assurance. They'd sat here at the large family table in the living area and talked them through the process. They suggested Elias and Darcie apply to permanently foster Lily first, with a view to eventual adoption. The lawyers believed they had a strong chance given Darcie's existing relationship with her. But looking at all the requirements again now, Darcie was far from reassured.

'I had no idea there were so many things we had to do.'

Security clearances. Full medicals. Training.

Her nerves tightened as she flicked page after page, listing every instruction, every requirement. They'd have to complete two foster parenting courses over a couple of months, meet with other prospective parents, do a paediatric first-aid course...

All the hoops meant it would take a minimum of four months before they could even go before the frankly intimidating interview panel that would decide whether or not they'd be approved as foster parents. It would be the biggest test of her life. She'd be quizzed by a bunch of strangers who would determine something so incredibly important and while she knew it was right that they have to do all the training, it felt like it was going to take forever. All she wanted was Lily—to be safe, to be with her so she could give her everything she'd missed out on.

'You haven't seen all these before?' Elias asked her curiously. 'Didn't you apply in the past?'

That lump in her throat grew and it hurt when she shook her head.

'Darcie?' He cocked his head. 'Why not?'

Because she'd known they'd decline her. The social worker had told her at the time that she had no chance.

But Elias looked astounded. 'You're ridiculously efficient and always prepared, Darcie. How have you not looked at this in much detail before now?'

She rubbed her forehead. He was so confident and such an over-achiever it would seem incomprehensibly stupid to him. 'Because some things are *so* important it becomes too hard to really try, do you know what I mean?' She glanced at him but of course he probably didn't get it. Her incompetence was embarrassing. 'If

I didn't know the details—the harsh reality—then I could still believe it might be possible. I could keep dreaming.'

He sat back, still frowning as he slowly nodded. 'So you avoided finding out for sure.'

Embarrassed, she nodded. 'Deluded myself with ignorance.'

He was silent, then spoke more softly. 'You didn't delude yourself, Darcie. You were scared because it means that much to you.'

'Means everything. Yes.' Her eyes filled because he did get it. 'But it might not work. It still mightn't.'

'Why would you think that?' he asked.

'After what had happened when she was taken…'

She'd been so scared off by the social worker that she hadn't even taken the forms to fill in. She'd been young and burned by the system herself so many times she just knew she'd never win back then. Truthfully she still didn't.

'What did happen?' He leaned closer, his gaze filled with concern as she remained silent. 'You know you can tell me anything, Darcie.'

Darcie wanted to believe him. She wanted to trust him. He'd sat there so calmly, looking so devastating in his jeans and tee. But she didn't talk about her past. People could never understand, and it made them uncomfortable. But she also knew she owed Elias some explanation because he'd been beyond supportive, and if they were to have any chance of succeeding then he needed to understand *Zara's* story more than her own.

'I met Zara when she came to the group home I was in. She was crazy, beautiful and kind, and we just hit it off. Other kids came and went but we stuck together. As soon as we were old enough we shared a tiny bedsit. I'd done well at school with computers, so I started in junior office jobs. Zara worked in clubs.' She paused. 'I'm sure you know the kind.'

'Clubs? Going clubbing...' he echoed the social worker.

'She was a dancer.'

'You mean an exotic dancer.'

Darcie lifted her chin. 'She was beautiful and fierce and she worked hard to look after Lily.'

'So did you.'

She saw the question in his eyes and knew exactly what he was wondering. 'She made good money whereas my entry-level office admin jobs initially were minimal pay. So yes, I tried dancing once. I hated every second and I was rubbish and I earned almost nothing. So I stayed in the offices working because I was quick at picking it up, good on computers, and

I progressed. But then Zara got pregnant. She thought Lily's father was going to save her.'

'He didn't.'

'Of course he didn't. I'd tried to tell her, tried to warn her. But she trusted so easily.'

'While you don't trust at all.' He regarded her sombrely.

'Once people have had what they want, they leave,' she said.

It had happened to her mother. It had happened to Zara. Darcie had been determined not to let it happen to her. But both Zara and her mother had left Darcie, too.

'I worked during the day and Zara looked after Lily and then I was there for Lily at night while Zara went back to working the clubs,' she said before Elias could ask her anything awkward. 'I didn't want her to but she was determined. She'd had her heart smashed so many times but she was such a dreamer.'

'You didn't have dreams, Darcie?'

'I was the realist. One of us had to be. But she thought she'd meet someone else…' She looked at him. 'Zara was hurt. We were all damaged in different ways but she'd suffered the worst. Don't judge her.'

'I'm not. You did what you had to do,' he said simply. 'And you did nothing wrong.'

'That's not what the social worker implied.'

She'd made her feel cheap and worthless and that she wasn't good enough to care for Lily.

'Everyone has things in their past that they're embarrassed about, or not proud of,' Elias said. 'If they don't let people have a few mistakes, then they wouldn't have *any* prospective foster parents.'

'I'm embarrassed about some things, but I'm not *ashamed*.' She blinked and looked him in the eyes. 'I'm proud of Zara and I'm proud of me. I'm proud of what I did and who I am and where I've come from. What I've overcome.' She smiled at him a little sadly. 'Maybe it wasn't ideal, but it worked. We survived and it was pretty okay. I was working my way up and we were saving for a new flat. But Zara got the flu. I didn't want her to go to work because she finished late and it was winter and cold but she insisted that she couldn't miss her shift or they'd replace her. She collapsed in the street on her way home.'

'Darcie—'

'It had got into her lungs,' she said hurriedly, needing to finish this last or she'd never be able to say it. 'It was so quick. Everything was *so* quick. They took Lily away that same day.'

'Oh, Darcie, I'm so sorry.'

It had been the absolute worst. In hours she'd lost everything. The social worker had been so condescending. They'd disregarded her arguments. She'd had to fight to find out where Lily even was and getting permission to visit—simply to stay in touch—had taken weeks. But she'd been determined to keep Zara's memory alive for Lily and determined to ensure Lily was as safe as she could be. She'd showered all the love she had to give on the girl each week. It was the highlight of her life.

She bit her lip. 'I thought I was so smart with the marriage plan. I thought it would make it easy—like be a magic wand or something. But I didn't appreciate how unrealistic it still really is.' Her eyes suddenly filled.

Elias took her hand in his and pressed it to his chest. She felt not just the warmth, but the firmness of his grip, the strength of muscle. It wasn't a sensual touch but supportive. He was literally solid and dependable and it was kind. It should have made her feel better. One tiny part did. But she was spiralling inside.

'You keep visiting Lily. I'll come, too. It'll strengthen your case.'

Wanly, she teased, 'You coming with me is going to make all the difference?'

'Absolutely.' He flashed a smile.

But she still couldn't smile back yet. 'This is too much to ask of you.'

'Because it's going to take longer than you hoped?'

'Because it's going to take more of everything. And even then there are no guarantees. We might fail.'

'That doesn't mean we quit before we've really begun. Not this time. No avoiding it anymore, Darcie. Because this does really matter. This is for Lily and we do this together. I want her to have a good home, too.'

'But I should be able to care for her without you having to do all this.'

Elias bit back the frustration roaring inside. His gut instinct was to fight—he wanted to help her and he didn't want her declaring that she didn't need him. For Darcie to have been so scared of failing that she couldn't draw on her usual capability shocked him. This wasn't the Darcie he knew—the capable woman who seemed unable to be broken. But of course she wasn't invincible. She'd just learned to mask her fears and work didn't matter to her anywhere near as much as this little girl did.

She was almost paralysed when facing the things she wanted most.

Now he understood her bond with Lily. Zara and Lily were her family and she'd have done anything to help them and she felt like she'd failed. He knew how that felt, too. He'd failed in his attempts to free his mother from his father's control. It all just made him want to help Darcie more.

'That's why you worked as hard as you did,' he said. 'Why you saved all your money.'

But he wondered about her early childhood. Why had she already been in the group home? Why hadn't her foster family placement worked out? What had happened to her birth parents? But he shelved the questions for now. He didn't want to push her—that she'd opened up as much as she had already this morning was something.

'I was good at spreadsheets. I could write reports. I learned I could earn more when I asked for it. It was how I could save for my freedom. And then for Lily.'

And she was right; that should be enough. Maybe it would have been—she'd not applied so she didn't know. She'd thought she needed a partner to project stability.

'And then you contacted Shaun.'

'I know you think I shouldn't have trusted him.' She looked at him. 'But don't judge him, either.'

He hadn't had much luck tracking that jerk down yet and hell, yes, he was judging him. He was also—horribly and unjustifiably—jealous. Even though he knew it was Zara who Shaun had loved. Even though he knew Darcie hadn't been intimate with any man other than himself.

Releasing a tight breath, Elias attempted to lighten the moment for them both. 'You know what you need?'

She gazed back at him blankly.

'Lunch. It's been a long, stressful morning and you need refuelling.'

It took him less than two minutes to empty packets onto a platter.

She chuckled as he placed it on the table. 'That looks amazing.'

The cheese and nut selection looked like little more than bar snacks to him, but he did know this about her. 'You like salty things, rich things.'

'Salty and rich?' She suddenly giggled as she snaffled some tamari almonds. 'You just described yourself.'

He was glad to see her wit slide back. 'And you like *me* very much.'

She rolled her eyes. 'Arrogance.'

'Truth,' he countered, and hit her with some more. 'And you need more than just a snack. Why don't you like actually dining with people, Darcie?' He watched her closely. 'What is it that scares you about that?'

She put the almond down and he saw that rebelliousness enter her eyes. 'Do you have to be so pointedly clever?'

It seemed calm Darcie had entirely disappeared.

'Don't feel sorry for me,' she muttered.

'I wouldn't be much of a human if I didn't feel for you, Darcie.'

'But I don't want your pity,' she breathed, her tone changing completely. 'You know that's not what I want from you.'

Oh, he knew. A sudden wave of anger swept through him, too. And rebellion turned to fire.

CHAPTER TWELVE

DARCIE HAD GOT LAZY. There was no denying it. In the week since they'd returned to London she'd spent more time relaxing than she ever had in all the rest of her life. Yes, she'd filled in all the foster application forms, arranged appointments for the checks required that she could so far, and she'd tried to track down Shaun— though she'd failed that latter. But she'd also slept in that large bed. Well, she'd not slept that much. She and Elias had other things to do in that bed. And she'd swum, lots. And now, yet again, she was having a hard time reining in the inappropriate direction of her thoughts. Never had she imagined she'd spend most of her mornings lying beside a luxurious heated pool watching a hunk of a man swim several lengths. Today, as it had every other day, her mouth dried while another part of her softened in readiness for his possession. She ached for it more and more. She didn't think she was ever going to tire of that delight.

'What are you thinking about?' Elias called to her from the water, teasing and husky and so, so hot.

He'd caught her staring—which hadn't exactly been hard seeing she couldn't seem to stop herself.

'Got an ache somewhere?' He pushed out of the water.

She nodded.

'Let me ease it for you.'

Thank goodness he seemed to share this rampant need right now. It was insatiable and the attempts to assuage it were so much fun. She'd never known physical pleasure could be like this. And she'd never known this kind of almost constant touch—never known how much she would adore it. Afterwards they lay on the day bed by the pool. His leg was pressed against hers, his hand holding hers. Their arms brushed and his breath warmed her shoulder. She'd never been the recipient of as much physical connection in all her life either. She'd thought herself quite insular before now. But maybe that was why now she had it she couldn't get enough. She *really* needed something else to occupy her mind—something other than Elias himself and other than her worry about Lily.

'This is bad,' she groaned. 'If I don't so something soon I'm never going to get my mojo back and I'll be this greedy sloth for ever.'

He looked down into her eyes. 'Would that be so bad?'

She chuckled. 'A little, yes. Maybe I should come back to work.'

He froze.

'What?' She laughed because she couldn't think what else to do in the face of that reaction. 'Would *that* be so bad?'

He smiled but it was forced. 'You can't want to come back to work, you *definitely* haven't had enough of a holiday.'

Because *work* was too bad? 'You know I liked working for you.'

'I don't want to be your boss again, Darcie.'

A finite tone. One she chose to ignore.

'You really think you had all power over me?' She shook her head. 'You know I could have got another job that paid as well, Elias.'

He sat back, his eyes widening. 'then why didn't you?'

'Because you thought you were so capable.' She suddenly chuckled. 'But you weren't completely. You know you never would have closed that Clarkson deal without me.'

'I *what*?'

'You know it's true. Who was it who came up with that killer concept?' She tilted her chin at him. 'Me. It was me.'

His mouth opened. She closed it with a nudge of her fingers to his chin.

'I liked working for you, Elias. You weren't

all that awful. You just had high expectations. Truthfully your worst failing was that you needed help and couldn't admit it.'

'I needed what?' He looked astounded. *'Help?'*

'You couldn't do it all on your own anymore,' she said, amused again by the strangled way in which he'd spoken. 'I enjoyed meeting the challenges you set. I liked it. You didn't abuse your power, Elias. You paid all of us well. You were never a bully. Honestly, working with you was stimulating.' She chuckled and waggled her brows at him because she didn't mean it in *that* way. Well, not entirely. 'I didn't resign because I didn't want to work with you anymore. It was only because I needed to support Shaun and I hoped I'd have the time to settle Lily in before she started school. But I was good at my job. So good you barely realised how much you'd come to rely on me.'

Elias watched the animation in her face and felt an easing of an uncomfortable load inside. Because maybe she was right? He hadn't talked through the deals with anyone the way he did with Darcie. And yes, he'd given her more and more responsibility because he'd known he could rely on her. She'd anticipated his require-ments because she'd understood exactly what he was trying to achieve. Sometimes she saw things he hadn't thought of. She was more than smart and she did hold her own with him…but she'd still not been completely honest. She'd not been able to be.

'I thought we worked pretty well together,' she said when he didn't say anything.

'I thought that, too. Which was why I was never going to risk jeopardising that with—'

'I know. But it's different now, isn't it?'

He stiffened. It was. But she didn't know the whole truth about his parents and why he couldn't be her boss now they were in a relationship. Because it was too messy, too easily abused. He wanted her to be free to say anything she wanted to him. That honesty meant more to him than anything. And he never wanted to take advantage of her. Never control her.

'You can't do it all on your own, Elias.' She lifted her chin. 'I bet you're missing me in there.'

He simply couldn't answer that honestly. 'What about a career of *your* own, Darcie?'

Her eyes flashed. 'I have a career. I'm good at what I do.'

'But you could do *anything*,' he countered. 'You didn't have the chance when you were younger, but you could study now if you wanted. Anything you like.'

'But I *liked* working with you.' She leaned

closer. 'Is this because of your dad cheating on your mum with his secretary?'

This was because of so much more than that. So much that he'd never said. The abusive coercion his father had wielded over them all—his secretary, his wife, his son.

'Because this wouldn't be like that, Elias. I know you wouldn't cheat—'

'No.' Of course he wouldn't.

This was about controlling. Not cheating.

He stood up from the day bed and ran his hand through his hair because he couldn't stand to remember it. 'Let's think about it some more.' He turned from the disappointment shadowing her eyes. 'We need to get ready for the visit with Lily.'

Truthfully, he was ambivalent about meeting Lily. Primarily he was going because he didn't want Darcie to go alone. Not again. She'd been alone a lot in her life and he understood isolation. Darcie had been alone through so much, for so long. He wanted her to get what she wanted—which meant he wanted Lily not to be alone, too.

It turned out Lily was a brown-eyed poppet with cocoa-coloured hair. From first glance he saw she was strikingly pretty. She was also shy. But the second the little girl spotted Darcie, she lit up. It was the one area in which he could totally relate to the child.

Then he saw Darcie light up too. Watching her with the girl made something in his bones ache. He'd never spent much time with kids. Never wanted to. Now he didn't have much choice and he needed to at least try. But it didn't come easily to him. He felt awkward and not even the encouraging approval shining in Darcie's eyes could make him feel completely good about it.

But the second visit he had his first genuine, easy interaction with Lily. He made her laugh by inadvertently acquiring an ice-cream moustache when they all had a cone from the truck at the park. Darcie had laughed, too, and the hit of pleasure within him had been insane. Making them both laugh had then become his mission. It had been surprisingly easy to achieve, simply by unleashing his inner idiot.

But after the fourth visit Darcie was uncharacteristically quiet on the drive home. As he followed her into the kitchen he thought through the afternoon. He'd thought it had gone well. They'd had a nice walk through the park; he'd spent some time pushing Lily's swing while Darcie spoke with the supervising social worker.

Now he watched her pour a glass of ice-water. 'What happened to make you upset? Did the social worker say something?'

She actually trembled and had to set the glass down before drinking any. She leaned against the bench, her head bowed, and his whole body ached with tension.

'It's going to take too long,' she said. 'The social worker said they might have to move Lily again.'

'Move her again?'

'To another foster home. She's in short-term placements.' She sighed deeply. 'I didn't want her to have to change places so often.'

Elias read the stiffness in her body. The agony she was suppressing. And he knew it ran deep. 'Is that what happened to you?'

He felt like he'd been stabbed when she didn't answer. But he didn't blame her. What right had he to pry into her painful past when he couldn't share his own? When he could hardly say anything of how he felt? Because talking about feelings—about history—had always led to hurt. But he needed to do better for Darcie. Now.

'My parents have an abusive relationship,' he blurted huskily. He ducked his head, unable to meet her eyes as she turned to him. 'I've never actually said that out loud before.'

Certainly he'd never told anyone.

'Elias—'

'My father is coercive,' he said quickly. Needing to just get it said. So she would know and possibly understand why he was the way he was. Why he found situations like this so difficult. 'He controls my mother. He always has. He tried to control me and for a while when I was a kid he succeeded.'

Darcie stepped towards him, but she didn't touch him. She just stood nearer. Elias turned his head slightly so he couldn't see the compassion blooming in her eyes. He couldn't stand to see that.

'He doesn't hit her,' he said with a rasp. 'But he's mean. He yells, berates, rages. So you're always on edge, you know? But then he's clever. He manipulates her—twists the facts and makes her think it's all her fault, that she caused the crisis. He's put her down for so long, he's been so entitled and so demanding and...' He rubbed his forehead and closed his eyes. 'I can't get her to leave him. I *want* her to leave him.'

He wanted that more than anything.

'But she won't,' he said. 'I don't think she ever will.'

He felt Darcie's hand on his arm. 'Elias...'

He shook his head jerkily. 'He did it to his secretary, too, you know? Controlled her. Used her. In the end she finally left but it took her more than a decade to gather the strength. He's a master of it.'

'And your mother?'

'He allowed her one child and wasn't it fortunate she gave him a son? Apparently I owed it to him to do everything he wanted. She was "lucky" he chose her and I was "lucky" to have him as my guide. Don't you know I'm just like him—smart and successful. I'm a natural leader and I should *always* insist on getting everything I want because it's my right, you know?' He spoke harshly, echoing the brash orders of his father who'd flared up at him time and time again. 'My birthright—my *duty*—was to be his heir in everything. I was to do exactly as he told me. Because mother and I would have nothing, and be nothing, without him.'

'But you left.'

'I had to.' And he'd left early, vowing never to be like that man. Never to lose control in the way that he did on the daily.

'And your mother? Do you see her at all?'

His heart shrank. 'A few times a year. I'm too successful for him to stop her from seeing me now. He needs to be able to brag. So he lets us meet. For her birthday, then mine. We have lunch together a week out from Christmas. Without him. Always without him.' He paused. Because he couldn't stand to be in the same room as that man. He couldn't—not without deteriorating into a raging mess of vitriol—because then he would be that man's equal and he couldn't ever allow that. So he remained distant and in control. Always. 'I ask her to come home with me. I tell her that if she wants to go somewhere—anywhere, anytime—I can make it happen. But she never says yes. I don't think she ever will. She's too broken.'

'I'm so sorry, Elias.'

He pressed his hands to his forehead, unable to look at her. Afraid, horribly afraid that he would fall apart if he did.

'She might yet.' Darcie's whisper was too sweet. 'It can take someone a long time to believe they can… But she knows you're there. You'll always be there for when, if, she's ever ready, right?'

He nodded jerkily. He knew all he could do was be there.

'And maybe…' Darcie sighed. 'Maybe seeing you is enough? Maybe there are other things in her life—while he's at work? I don't know much, Elias, other than that things are often so complicated. Sometimes so hard to understand.'

'Yeah.' And coercion was horrifyingly scary and difficult to escape. The only person Elias wanted to control was himself. Yet he was losing it, wasn't he? Even here. Now. 'I don't want to…'

He couldn't say it aloud—that worst fear of his. But he didn't want to be like that man. But he might.

Because he liked touching Darcie too much. He tried to tell himself that need wasn't a symptom of possessiveness but simply the need for connection—to touch her somewhere, anywhere—even just the light pressure of her knee against his thigh as they sat beside each other. But *needing* a physical link wasn't something he'd experienced before and to find it irresistible—to feel the silkiness of her skin, her warmth, the softness and the strength. He savoured every time he sank into the deliciousness of her body.

But the need was now more than sexual. When she was gone from the room he chilled and ached with emptiness. He'd become like a damned pack animal that always needed to lie in contact with its mate—seeking solace, and comfort in the knowledge he only had to move a mere millimetre to feel her. It was a comfort he'd never known he liked. And he liked to *hear* her admit she wanted him. He liked to hear that over and over. Since when was he so *needy*? Wasn't that controlling, too? He couldn't allow this to turn into an obsession. He didn't want to turn into his father. So somehow he needed to ensure Darcie kept her freedom—even from him. *Always.*

Darcie didn't know what else to say, how else to help him. The trembling of his fingers gave away the deep well of emotion he'd exposed. Of course he was upset. He was *human*. He couldn't deny that. But she understood now how he tried—why it was that he rarely opened up, rarely expressed emotion. No wonder he never raised his voice, never showed strong feelings. No wonder he tried to remain at a distance and never let relationships last more than a few weeks at most. He'd been scarred by his parents. And was scared of becoming something else.

The day they'd married had been the one time she'd seen him visibly lose control of his emotions—when it wasn't cool disapproval but white-hot fury that had rolled off him. His re-actions had been driven by that rage. She still didn't understand why he'd felt it so strongly. But he'd recovered himself quickly and worked through, deciding that their merger—mar-riage—was a good one. She wanted to help him now.

'This is why you're so focused on work,' she said.

He dropped his hands and a soft, weary chuckle emerged. 'You love work, why can't I?'

'You used it to get your independence.'

'Yeah. Sound familiar?' He lifted his head and looked at her. 'I wanted to earn enough to take her away and give her a damned palace, if that's what she wanted. But she didn't want it. She wouldn't leave him. I don't know if she ever will.'

Darcie's heart broke for him. 'Relationships are complicated,' she said. 'I've never really understood them all that well.'

'Ditto.' His lips twisted. 'Work is the outlet for my own controlling tendencies.'

She shook her head. 'You don't have controlling tendencies. You're not like him, Elias.'

'You don't know that,' he said painfully.

'I do,' she whispered.

But some of those things his father had tried to drill into him *were* true—Elias was smart, successful, a natural leader. And he did often get what he wanted. But because he *worked* for respect, not by bullying others into it.

'I've worked alongside you for *years*,' she added. 'More than long enough to know you're not manipulative. You're not coercive. You're not a bully. Not in any way. You never even yell at anyone.'

He inspired his employees. He didn't harangue them. Yes, he had high expectations—but the highest he saved for himself.

He sighed and bent his head again. 'Don't be kind, Darcie.'

'I'm being honest.' She brushed the backs of her fingers against his tense jaw. 'You should let yourself have more, Elias. *So* much more than just work.'

'Work is a good challenge. Safe.'

'There could be other challenges, too.'

'No. It's enough. It's all I need.'

No, he needed—and should have—so much more than that. Just as she should have more, too. Her heart ached for him because she knew what it was like not to have had a home that was a safe haven. Not to have had a loving family. And it couldn't be fixed. There was nothing she could say that could magically make this all better. It was what it was, and she knew that moving forward took slow processing, slow progress. So she stepped back.

'You know what you *need*?' She nudged his shoulder with her own.

He looked at her in query.

'Refuelling.'

He laughed briefly and shook his head. 'You know I'm bigger than you. I can't subsist on cashews and camembert...'

'Subsist?' she mock-screeched. 'Yeah, well, I mightn't be able to cook but I can reheat every bit as well as you do.'

They'd been heating assorted Michelin-starred meals all week. She figured it was her turn to use the microwave. It didn't take a moment to put one of the packs into the microwave and while the machine was humming she fossicked through the linen, silver and glassware the designers had stocked the cupboards with.

Elias watched her with mild bemusement. 'Are you actually setting the table?'

'Yeah, quick, do you want to take a photo?' she quipped tartly.

His smile flashed. She set the plates down on the placemats and they both picked up their forks. The food had been ordered in from another Michelin restaurant and melted in her mouth. She'd never had this kind of nourishment when growing up. She'd never had *any* of this before. And maybe Elias needed to understand that, too—to know why helping Lily was so important to her. And to let him know she understood something of the stress he'd felt in his own family.

'Dinnertime is such a happy family cliché,' she said softly. 'And I never fitted in to a happy family picture.' She inhaled. 'My father walked out before I was even born. My mother made it only a few months before handing me in to a refuge. I must have been…' She shrugged with the echo of hopelessness she'd long ago felt. 'I don't know what I was or why it was that I couldn't seem to last with one family for more than a year.' She swallowed. 'Some tried. Some were clearly just collecting the fee. One had their own daughter who was a similar age and when I did better at her in school, they decided I was too difficult and would be better off with a family that could give me the attention I needed.'

'But you didn't get it?'

She shook her head. She'd taken the thing that had made her stand out—her schooling— and pushed it as far as she could as long as she could alone. 'I was put into another couple of short placements that might possibly go permanent, but it was just more dinner table awkwardness. It's supposed to be intimate, right? The time when people—families, friends, couples—connect. When they talk and show they care about each other and they communicate.' It was when love was shown, was built, solidified. 'But when you're not really wanted, when you're sitting there but you're so out of place and uncomfortable and...'

'It became something you avoided.' He nodded. 'Because you were missing out on something seemingly simple, but that should have meant much.'

Yeah. It had been something she'd wanted

for so long and had never got. So she'd stopped trying to get close to anyone much. She avoided those social things and buried herself in work.

'I went into a group home. I got a part-time job after school and then I wasn't at the house for dinner. I was working.'

Elias put his hand over hers. 'I didn't love dinner at the table much, either. We got to listen to my father lecture me on how like him I was, how I was to follow in his footsteps. He berated my mother on the areas in which she needed to improve. Those were the good nights. Others were more volatile. Smashed plates and spilled wine.'

Darcie flipped her hand and locked her fingers with his. 'We could make dinnertimes for Lily very different. Very much better.'

'Yeah, one thing's for sure, we're going to need to employ a cook.' He grinned.

She chuckled back at him.

But Elias's expression turned sombre and he looked at her intently. 'You shouldn't have this burden.'

'Lily's not a burden.'

'I didn't just mean Lily.'

'Other people have far more to burden them.'

'Other people have far more support. You should've had people in your corner. People helping you get everything you should have had...you could have done anything.' He drew breath. 'But now you can. Now you have me.'

A flush heated her skin. She slipped her hand free and stood on the pretext of getting another glass of water. Because she didn't have him, really—not for long.

'Is it really so unfathomable that someone would want to go the extra mile for you, Darcie?'

She kept her back to him. She simply didn't know how to answer that.

Only then she sensed he was right behind her. He put his hands on her shoulders and his voice was quiet and gentle as he drew her back against him. 'I'm sorry you've been alone for so long.'

'Some things don't have easy fixes, I guess. Sometimes they don't have fixes at all.'

She closed her eyes and softened, allowing herself to rest on him. Because this sharing and this support... It worked both ways. Even if it was only for now. Because 'now' was all there ever really was.

'I'm sorry your dad's such a jerk,' she mumbled. 'And I'm sorry your mum can't leave him. Yet.'

'Are we cancelling each other out in the pity stakes?'

She chuckled weakly and turned to him. 'I think so.'

He framed her face in his hands. 'I guess that just leaves this.'

Emotion thundered through her as she gazed up at him. It left so much more than *this*, than lust. There was trust, there was care, there was *wonder*…and there was such sweet possibility. But he was pale and intense and so devastating, and he seemed to have frozen as he stared right into her eyes. She read confusion in his. Uncertainty even. He was, she realised, vulnerable. So she rose on tiptoe and pressed her lips to his.

'Darcie?' The huskiest whisper broke her apart.

'I'm here,' she breathed.

'Yes.' He melted, instantly. His hands spanned her waist, holding her to him.

But she pressed closer still, instinctively certain that he needed more. He, too, was lonely and right now he was unguarded—close to icing back up. She didn't want that. She wanted him to have it all. He, too, needed to be shown—to be gifted—love. And as she pushed, he stepped backwards until he rested his butt against the edge of the table. She pushed his chest and he let her—leaning right back, sliding onto the large wooden expanse. She breathed out at the sight of him there before her and then climbed astride him. She shifted clothes—unbuttoning his, shedding only what was required of hers to give them both access to those secret, heated, aching parts that could make them come together—whole.

'This is a much better use for the table.' He groaned. 'But I don't have anything—'

'I do.' She pulled the protection from where she'd put it in her pocket first thing this morning.

'Confident, capable Darcie,' he muttered with a strained half smile as he took it from her. 'Prepared.'

Yes, she was ready for him. She wanted him. Always. She kissed him deeply and felt the quake in his body as she poured everything into the caress. She needed to show him. To make him feel the way he made her feel—so content. And so complete.

'Let me help.' She pushed his hands to the side but hers were shaking almost as badly as his had. So she paused and let her mouth work him instead. The scent of him, the taste, the straining arousal made her own need surge. Having him like this—all steel, yet velvety and vulnerable—he was hers for the claiming. He was just hers. And she was his. For once she truly felt as if she had her person—the one to whom she truly belonged.

'Darcie!' A growl of warning, and of submission.

He put his hands on her hips and lifted her away only to reposition her so she was fully astride him before quickly finishing the job of protecting them both. And then, with her right there in place astride him, he let his fingers tease her until she was the one to growl again.

'My turn,' she snapped. Gazing down into his eyes, she swiftly sank and took him deep. 'Mine.' Moaning in pleasured relief, she smoothed her hands over his strong, broad chest and pinned him in place. 'Elias.'

'Darcie…' He released a shocked gasp as he shuddered. 'I can't hold back.'

'Good.' Because she didn't want him to. Besides, nor could she. She rocked, riding him harder and faster, feeling the power as he rippled beneath her. He was hers. To feast on. To pleasure. To take. The man she understood. The man she wanted.

The man she *loved*.

CHAPTER THIRTEEN

THE NEXT MORNING Darcie woke later than usual. She took longer in the shower—distracted by the intensity and direction of her own thoughts. They were all on Elias, of course. On that profound moment they'd had last night. The moment that had extended when he'd carried her up to the bedroom and they'd silently, frantically, come together again. Then again. It was different than before—more physical, raw and uncontrolled. And it had been incredible. But on waking this morning, it was the first thing that entered her mind. The truth. She'd fallen utterly, irrevocably in love with him and now she longed for *everything*.

She pressed her hands to her chest, as if she could hold her poor heart together, as she considered all that had happened. All so quickly. He'd accompanied her on several visits with Lily now. They usually walked to the park not far from her current foster home. They played together on the swings and slide; ate an ice cream if the truck was there. It was the simplest of pleasures for both Darcie and Lily and she liked to hope Elias, too. His blossoming ease had taken her by surprise. He was gentle with Lily, interested, and he could make her giggle. Darcie, too. And he was just present—strong, supportive, with that half smile that always made her spirits lift. Unsurprisingly Lily was as bowled over by him as everyone else always was. Darcie recognised that eagerness to please him, to attract his attention. Elias was an impressive figure, but he was not intimidating to Lily. Not when he crouched down and greeted her each time with that charm and that increasing softening in his demeanour that she'd never seen in the office. He was a natural and he would be such a wonderful caregiver for Lily. For any other children, too. He was strong and successful, yes, but he was also deeply sensitive. He just hid it mostly and so very well. Because he, too, had been wounded. He, too, was wary of emotion.

As Darcie absently let the shower rain down, she ached for everything *impossible*. Because she knew that while he, like she, had never wanted to marry, his reasoning was different. Where she'd been afraid of being abandoned, he was afraid of being awful. Yet he couldn't be further from that. But he constrained his emotions and was clearly determined to keep distance from others. *All* others. Even lovers. And he *would* tire of her eventually. Because he was quick in mind and always hungry. To him this was just another project and once it was complete, he would grow restless. He would move on to the next. But after last night *her* stance had shifted. She wanted more. Sure, she'd felt him shaking in her arms. He'd swooped upon her and all but devoured her. He'd wanted her intensely and she suspected he *still* wanted her. Just not enough.

Darcie had never had anyone stay for her. Nor had she ever had a place where she'd been invited to stay for good. She'd never had her parents. She'd never had a permanent home. She'd found Zara, but lost her too soon. She'd lost Lily, too. Even Shaun and the others in that last home. She'd always had to move—*nothing* had ever lasted. She'd been rejected or abandoned repeatedly and all she knew for sure was that she was not having any of that happen to Lily. It would stop with her. So she had to be so very careful now. She couldn't ruin this. Not by asking for too much from Elias—for pushing too hard and expecting too much. Because it wasn't for her. It wouldn't be. But she could ensure Lily had it all.

'You're not going in to the office today?' she asked him as lightly as she could when she finally made it downstairs.

He'd not gone into the office much at all this week. He'd taken one of the rooms on the second floor and set up his computers, but even so he hadn't been in there often. Now he was seated at that large dining table—the one she couldn't look at without feeling a sensual quiver—taking his time over his coffee and toast.

'Apparently marriage is making me lazy, too,' he answered wryly.

'Don't forget this isn't a real marriage,' she muttered beneath her breath.

'But Darcie…' He shot her a look from the top of his mug. 'We have the certificate. We've consummated it. We live together…if it walks like a duck, quacks like a duck, then I think we can safely call it a duck.'

'Yes, but it's a *rubber* duck,' she said stoutly. 'As in not real. It only exists for Lily.'

'Right. It's vital for Lily that you and I share a bed and sleep very little while in there…'

This was one tease she couldn't quite handle. 'That's also a temporary thing. It's an education for me.'

'An education?' He half laughed, half choked on the coffee. 'And what do you think it is for me?'

She truly didn't know and she didn't really want to ask. She felt too unstable, so instead she tried to deflect with a joke of her own. 'An added extra? Bonus?'

'A perk of the job?' His smile faded.

Darcie awkwardly poured herself a mug of coffee. Not that she needed it. She already felt wired—wary. As if everything was going too well. Their set-up was now too lovely and too fragile to be true. And it wasn't true, of course. Which is why she'd just reminded herself. And she did again mentally—*it's not a real marriage.*

But that didn't stop her from wanting to keep it—not just to stay in his bed but to stay with *him* for good. Yes, she wanted this delight of a marriage to become real. But life didn't work like way. Things changed. Always. People left. She knew that and yet somehow still she'd fallen deeply, deeply in love with him. Desperately she took a large sip of the too-hot coffee. Because of course she loved him. How could she not? He was smart and challenging and considerate and bold and—

'I thought I'd go sort out some things from my flat this morning,' she mumbled. It was a weak excuse, but the only one she could think of.

'Need some help?'

She shook her head and left the room. She needed space to get her head back together and her careering emotions under control.

Forever only happened in fairytales. She knew there was only *now* and there was never, *ever* certainty. She knew that better than anyone. And yet again she made herself remember. Elias had been very clear—this wasn't going to last. It was an interlude. So as lovely as it was, she wasn't going to ruin it by professing her love for him. He'd be mortified and he'd pity her more than he already did and she really didn't want him to linger any more than he should if he felt some horrible responsibility for her emotionally as well as financially now. That would be terrible.

So she'd play it light and soon enough he'd give her one of those bracelets from the stock in that second drawer in his safe. His 'goodbye, lover' gift. Plus the house. Plus Lily... And she would hold her head high and stay calm. Stay silent.

Only part of her didn't want to stay silent anymore. She'd got used to speaking her mind with him. To demanding—if not simply taking—what she wanted. As she had last night. And she didn't want to stop. But to tell him this would wreck everything.

Her greediness was too much—yet hot anger bubbled, mixing with bitterness. Why did she always miss out? Why couldn't she get it all? After all, it wasn't so very much, was it? Merely an intangible.

The thing was, she knew he'd give her anything *material* that she asked for. But the unseen, ephemeral things—like trust and unconditional love—he wouldn't give her those. He wouldn't give *anyone* those. And she didn't blame him. So she'd keep her secret to herself. She'd make the most of each magic moment she had with him in this short time. She would keep her heart as safe as she could.

Elias couldn't stop thinking about Darcie. She'd been gone for a while and he missed her. Too much. It was *all* too much. He'd thought that the last week would have been enough to sate the desire between them. But it hadn't. Maybe the fact that he'd wanted her for so long, and suppressed it for so long, had made it stronger. Maybe it was because they were married. Maybe that super quick, flashy ceremony had somehow created something stronger than they'd intended. But that was impossible. In reality it was no more substantial than the thin paper that it was printed on and it could be easily burned away to little more than a few cinders. Yet still it felt like there was a bond building—like steel cord tethering them together. He wanted her to be happy. He wanted to help her with Lily. He wanted everything for her.

She'd been so serious, suppressing so much of her natural vitality, for the time she'd worked for him because she'd had to. She'd had burdens most people wouldn't cope with. Now she needed joy and laughter, fun and above all *freedom*. Not to have to work all the time. Not to have such responsibilities all the time. Not to be constantly afraid that everything was going to come crashing down. Because seeing these glimpses of her—laughing Darcie, natural and free and so beautiful, it meant everything.

It's not a real marriage.

She'd said that so softly, yet so intensely. As if, if she repeated it often enough it would remain true. As if she were reminding herself. And instead of agreeing like he ought to, there was a rebellious—okay, petulant—streak that had wanted to argue with her. For one mad moment he'd wished it really *were* real.

But *she* didn't want it to be real—hence those reminders. And perhaps it couldn't be real because they'd never been on the same plane. Never on an equal footing. They'd been out of balance the whole time they'd known each other.

She'd had no real choice but to do as he'd wished when she'd been his employee. She'd had to work because she'd been saving money to care for Lily. Even though, yes, she'd held her own with him and helped him more than he'd previously acknowledged, in the end he'd still been her boss. He'd still had far more power than her. And then—in their physical intimacy—he'd had the power then, too, right? He'd had the experience. Except for last night when she'd devastated him.

Since their wedding the floodgates had opened and he couldn't close them again. His emotions were at sea, the craving uncontrollable. He'd go away for a few hours and think he had himself back together but five minutes in her company and he was undone all over again, unable to stop all sorts of feelings, desires, memories assailing him. He wanted it all to stop.

His father had cheated. His father was controlling. His father had insisted on him following him into the family business. He'd told him again and again that he'd raised him to be just like him—a winner, all-powerful, in control of all. In the end Elias had fought hard to leave and he tried hard never to look back because he knew he'd failed his mother in being unable to help her escape. In convincing her that she even needed to—to recognise that what was going on was so damaging to them all.

But being with Darcie brought up feelings he'd forgotten. Feelings he'd not known before. But worst of all were the fears that things that had happened in the past might happen again.

Yet he couldn't resist her. And he certainly couldn't leave her.

They'd married to secure Lily's future—it was meant to have been little more than an arrangement. And while it had turned into more, she didn't *love* him. Yes, she felt desire. Gratitude. Amusement. But not love. And he knew that in their current situation, she didn't have the freedom to find out whether deeper feelings could blossom. For him they had. But everything was tangled and he couldn't trust what he thought was building between them and he certainly couldn't admit how he was feeling. Because it would make her feel all the more obligated towards him. She'd been denied support and caring and companionship for so long her response would bloom bigger because of that deficit.

So he needed to do the opposite. He needed to keep these burgeoning feelings to himself while somehow ensuring she achieved absolute autonomy. Because maybe if she knew she had complete independence—financially, emotionally—then that freedom would enable her to figure out the decisions *she* truly wanted to make. Maybe she could figure out how she really felt. Even about him. He had to gift her everything somehow. He decided to go in to the office— get a little space to see if that would help him think more clearly. Because he couldn't work out how he could do it for her. How could he set her free when it was the very last thing he wanted to do?

CHAPTER FOURTEEN

LATE IN THE afternoon Elias found Darcie back at the table that he couldn't look at without remembering being flat on his back with her all but naked and astride him. Now she was clad in threadbare blue jeans and faded tee—some of the clothes she'd retrieved no doubt—nibbling on a wedge of brie cheese and just like that he couldn't think. But then he'd spent all afternoon thinking. Planning. Now he had to put it into action. But before he could speak she jumped from her seat.

'We're going to have Lily for an at-home visit!' She came close and slid her hands up his chest. 'The social worker phoned. She's really positive about how things are going and this is a *massive* step, Elias!'

'That's wonderful news.' Yet at the same time his heart sank beneath her touch. But she was so effervescent and kissed him with such enthusiasm he almost lost his head completely. He jerked away, trying to get his brain back.

Darcie blinked and froze but Elias barely noticed. He'd formulated a plan. A good one. He'd gone back to basics. To business. To the language they both understood. And he had to

present the case now while he could still remember to.

'I have something for you,' he said.

'Oh?' She stared at the envelope he held
tightly. 'What is it?'

His heart thumped as he handed it to her and
she pulled the paperwork out.

'It's a postnuptial agreement,' he said, too
impatient to give her the chance to read it for
herself. 'Seeing we didn't have time to arrange
things before we got married.'

It had been uncharacteristically reckless of
him not to have all the details finalised before
they'd married but all that had mattered at the
time was making things right for her in that
moment. He'd not considered the complexities,
not realised the ramifications. Now he did. But
it wasn't too late to straighten things out. He
watched, his muscles tightening, as she scanned
the document silently, quickly flicking through
the pages, assimilating and understanding the
text.

Finally she lifted her head and looked at him
directly. 'Why are you doing this?'

Elias paused as he saw the coolness in her
blue eyes.

'I'm not a charity case,' she added before he
could answer.

That tone chilled him. Automaton Darcie was

back. Only not quite—there was still emotion in her eyes. Except it wasn't an emotion he'd wanted to see.

He cleared his throat, suddenly wary. 'Lily is.'

She shook her head dismissively. 'But I don't need you to do this. I can take care of her myself if you don't want to be involved.'

He recoiled. 'If I don't...' He paused and drew a breath. He'd not made his thinking clear. 'Darcie. This is for *you*.' It was to free her completely. 'We should have arranged this before the wedding but we didn't have time. You know this makes sense.'

But her face whitened. 'How does it make sense?'

He took a couple of short breaths, increasingly on alert and suddenly unsure of how to proceed. But he'd not gone about this quite right. He'd sprung it on her and she wasn't comprehending why. 'Because this way you never have to worry about being able to care for Lily again. And *she'll* never have to worry. Lily's lost enough. Now she won't lose more. She won't lose *you*. You wanted to protect her from that, right?'

Darcie said nothing.

'You know I'm in a position to be able to do this,' he added. 'This is nothing to me.'

She shifted suddenly, turned away from him.

Uncertainty stabbed. But Darcie was the one person in the world who'd been Lily's constant and this was for Darcie, too. Because it wasn't Lily he saw in his mind. It was Darcie herself. Darcie as a child, desperately wishing—waiting—for a family, for a place to belong. Moving from one to another and it never working out. Trying to be unobtrusive. Trying to stay safe. Ending up avoiding getting too involved with any of those people because she didn't want to be hurt anymore. Hiding her true self and doing only what she thought she ought to. She wanted better for Lily. But he wanted better for *her*.

He wanted her to feel safe and secure and by ensuring Lily's financial future, she would be able to be honest with him. Able to explore whatever feelings were there…

'I don't want you to do this,' she said briskly, keeping her back to him. 'I'm not going to sign it.'

Were there feelings there? If there were, he'd just hurt them. And he'd done it too easily. Too thoughtlessly. His own defences rose.

'Are you the only one who's allowed to help her? Isn't that a kind of arrogance of its own, Darcie?'

She whirled to face him. The emotion swirling in her eyes transfixed him. He stared, waiting, willing her to say what was on her mind.

He *needed* that from her. He needed the truth—her free to tell him anything. Whatever was on her mind. Without fear. Without coercion. That was the whole point of this.

'In my experience,' she said, her tone brittle, 'people don't tend to follow through on their promises.'

'Right.' He breathed through the ache in his chest because he knew then that she didn't trust him. 'Which is why this is a legal and enforceable contract. It's why you're getting all the money you're going to need up-front. So you have full security.'

She shook her head and he finally understood the full gamut of emotion in her eyes. It was hurt. It was disappointment. And it was rejection.

'It's only money,' he said gruffly. 'You know I have more than I need.' But futility rose. He wasn't used to people not accepting the things he offered and this was the most important thing he could offer anyone, and he couldn't stop himself from trying to convince her again. 'This is your freedom, Darcie. You won't have to worry about money again. Work if you want, but you won't have to. You'll be able to care for Lily however you want. This is the one thing I can do with any certainty of success. It's nothing to me.'

She looked as if he'd just shot her.

'Nothing,' she echoed.

That bad feeling overwhelmed him. This had been a mistake. She was taking this all wrong. He'd screwed up in such a stupid, obvious way. He never should have got the whole massive legal document drawn up, the funds assigned, everything—without even *talking* to her first. He'd not learned—and he should have learned that from buying the bloody house. Even though she'd loved it, he'd still done it without consulting her. And if he couldn't learn from something that basic, would he only regress the longer they were together? Would he eventually be everything his father was? Not just controlling—making every tiny decision with such autocratic arrogance, but manipulative and mean to boot.

He couldn't take the risk. He couldn't stand it if he did that to Darcie, to Lily.

'The *one* thing you can do?' she said, bitterness sharpening every word. 'Elias, you've *married* me. You've got a team of lawyers and advisers working round the clock and now you're offering me millions…that's all a little more than *one* thing.'

But it wasn't enough. It wasn't what she wanted. And he knew then that he could never, ever give her what she wanted. What she needed. What she deserved. She was better off without him. She and Lily both were. Because he would never get this right. It wasn't in his blood.

Darcie couldn't believe what she'd read in that paperwork. What he was offering. And the degree to which he was freezing on her now. But she knew *why* he was doing something so extreme. He'd had enough. He was finalising things so he could exit stage left and he was doing it on a grand scale because he felt *sorry* for her. This was her version of the jewellery he gave his dates—his parting gift. Only for her it was wads of cash. Did she get the extra big pay-off for giving him her virginity? Her bitterness washed over her in a vitriolic wave of acidity.

'Darcie,' he breathed out harshly. 'If you sign this then it doesn't matter what happens between us.'

Exactly. They could break up. He could leave and not have to worry—not have to think about her ever again.

'We fight? We fall out?' he said briskly. 'I can't withhold the money and Lily's security is assured. And you can be completely honest with me.'

Of course he thought they'd fight and fall out and he was prepping for the moment. Obviously he expected it to be soon. Well, it was going to be sooner than even he realised.

'You think I'm not completely honest with you now?' she asked.

She saw his hesitation and it appalled her. Did he know? Had he guessed that her feelings for him had changed—had deepened? How mortifying was that?

'I think you bit your tongue a million times in the last two years,' he said, his frustration audible. 'You "behaved" because you couldn't afford for me to fire you. I don't want you curbing your instincts because you're worried about me walking out on you. I want your honesty, Darcie. More than anything.'

Honesty was all he wanted. Not love. He didn't want that. Well, the truth would be excruciating for him to hear. She'd fallen in love with him and he was planning his escape from her—expecting her to happily agree to his over-the-top plan. As if she could *ever* be satisfied with this?

'You know I didn't have to handle you so very much,' she said. 'But I think you're almost as untrusting as I am if you think you have to *pay* for my honesty.' This felt so transactional. That if she didn't sign he wouldn't trust her to tell him the truth. That he was so wary spoke volumes. She'd thought they'd built a different, deeper relationship. But they hadn't. Or at least *he* didn't feel any such change. Whereas *she* couldn't curb any instincts or emotions around him anymore. That ability had disappeared in a flash. Which meant she needed to get out of here. *Now*. Before she revealed it all.

'I still want you to sign it,' he said doggedly. He stood, inflexible, his expression shut down—he was Elias of the boardroom and he didn't negotiate.

Too bad for him.

'That's not going to happen.' She met his gaze directly, summoning all her years of masking her feelings to hold herself together for just a little longer. 'Not ever.'

But she saw the flicker of emotion in his eyes. Then the cooling. The *steeling*. And she knew he'd gone.

'You want to do this on your own,' he said. Then he nodded. 'That's probably for the best.'

He was backing away from her but she needed to beat him to it. She needed to stop him from saying stupid platitudes and trying to be kind. *She* needed to avoid all that humiliation. She needed to *run*.

'You don't actually need me, Darcie,' he said. 'You don't need anyone.'

Maybe that was true. But she'd *wanted* him with her. She didn't want to lose what she thought they'd shared. And people did *need* other people. Humans weren't designed to be alone. They were social creatures who thrived better in groups. In *families*. She yearned for that fulfilment. For everything. She still wanted it all even when she'd never really believed she'd get it. And she wanted it for Lily. But Elias didn't—he didn't recognise that it even existed. She was never going to get it from him.

'I'm sorry I got you involved in all this.' She tossed the papers onto the table. 'It's a mess. But we both knew it was never going to last.'

His shoulders lifted but his gaze didn't leave hers. She watched the stiffness consume him. The suppression of emotion—or maybe that was still her wishful thinking. Because there was no emotion now. He was Elias of old—cold, clinical, controlled.

'You'll get Lily. I know you will,' he said. 'And I'll always do everything I can for you both. If you ever need anything, all you have to do is ask.'

She never would. She didn't want him to do anything else. Not now. She was just an unwanted obligation. A responsibility he'd never wanted. That realisation was her worst nightmare. She glanced about, seeking her escape, realising just how hollow and empty this house was.

'I can't stay here.' The admission leaked out. Not in this place she'd thought might finally be her home. The place where she'd hoped she might have a whole family. It was too huge. Too full of unrealised dreams.

'No, please stay. At least let me give you that.' He looked at her sombrely. 'At least for tonight. I'll leave. I'll go to the penthouse. Give you some space.'

His cool, oh-so-sensible decision struck like a sword to her heart. Giving her space? That was him being *kind*.

Too bad. She was leaving, too. She was *never* staying here even one more night. Because she couldn't stand it. Why was it always her? What was the defect within her that meant people left and she was unloved? Why would she never, ever be good enough?

Darcie did the only thing she could. She turned her back and left.

And Elias didn't even try to stop her.

CHAPTER FIFTEEN

ELIAS SPENT THE best part of the next forty-eight hours convincing himself he'd done the right thing. Because he'd done what she'd asked—therefore that *had* to be the right thing. He wasn't standing in her way. He'd let her go—which was what she'd wanted. He wasn't trying to control her in any way. So why did he feel so damn terrible inside?

He'd always known that Lily and Darcie both deserved more than he could ever offer them—not just those material things, or even the emotional things. They deserved someone who actually wanted the *same* things they did. He'd never wanted a family—not some big home with a rambling garden, and a child's sports or dance practices tying up time every weekend. He certainly didn't want the burden of responsibility for someone's emotional growth and development. He wasn't ever going to be good at it and he loathed failure more than anything.

Except he'd enjoyed those too-few hours at the playground with Lily. He'd already been thinking about swimming lessons and seeing her enjoy that pool at the big home he'd bought before he'd even met her. The home that was now unbearably empty without the energy, laughter, vibrancy and sheer force of life that was Darcie. The home that mocked him with that big dining table. Not to mention the ostentatious diamond ring and solid gold band that she'd left behind on it. But he would only disappoint her even more the longer they remained involved. There'd be a slow decay as resentment built because he couldn't be all she needed. But it was at that point in his ruminations that Elias's inner arrogance emerged.

You could be.

He *didn't* want to be another person who'd abandoned her or who'd just disappeared from her life. He'd wanted to be better than that. He wanted to help her still—however he could. And so he would—by finishing the jobs he'd begun. While she'd *asked* for it to be over, he couldn't leave those things just yet. He still wanted her to have everything and he'd be there as backstop. He'd wanted her to know she had all the choices and that's what he'd strived to do. He'd tried to gift her everything—without her having to ask for it all.

But she'd made the choice she'd wanted. She'd chosen to leave him.

And why was that? Why didn't she want him? The horror of her rejection burned like acid and made anger rise. He'd been such a fool. Clumsy and bossy and uncommunicative. Why hadn't she understood his intention?

Because you never truly told her.

In truth, he realised, *she'd* run away before he could. And she was avoiding him now. She'd not responded to his message checking she was okay, making it clear it wasn't his business to know anymore.

But his heart begged to differ.

Darcie couldn't miss her visit with Lily. Even though she was heartbroken and struggling to hide it, she needed to show up for the little girl. She was never letting Lily experience that feeling of being let down, not ever from her. Fortunately the playground was busy and Lily was keen to race up and down the slide, needing little help from Darcie. It was enough for her just to be there.

'Elias is busy with work,' she'd explained briefly to both Lily and the social worker. She'd need to work on a better explanation when it came to revising the application forms, but she'd deal with that in a day or so. It was enough to get through today.

'Yes, he explained.' The social worker had smiled. 'But it's good he's able to do some of the modules online, though. So he won't fall behind.'

Darcie had stilled, then quickly nodded as if she'd known all along that had been his intention. But her lungs were still constricted and she was forced to take shorter breaths. Elias was still completing some of the foster parent training modules? Why would he want to? Was it simply because the man didn't like leaving things unfinished or did he still want to be involved in some way? It had been obvious he'd come to like Lily and that he'd wanted the best for her as Darcie did. But surely now they were no longer together he didn't need to do that? And had he actually gone away? Where to? For how long? For the first time in years Darcie didn't know his schedule and she hated it.

That night she couldn't sleep. Again. Her small bed seemed so empty, her room so silent. She missed the heat, the closeness, the soft laughter in the small hours when they teased each other. She missed *him*. Terribly. And as she lay, wakeful and her mind whirring, a shaft of uncertainty pierced through the fierce armour she'd been trying to knit back together. Why *was* he still doing the training if he'd been so determined to ensure Darcie had complete financial independence and thus could care for Lily alone?

What if she was somehow wrong about that? But how else could she take that horrible postnuptial contract? It had assumed an end to their marriage after all, hadn't it? Though what if he'd not meant to push them away quite so soon?

She struggled to remember his expression when he'd handed her the paperwork. Had he meant for it all to be over then and there? Or could she have had even just a little longer as his lover? But if she'd stayed, if she'd accepted less, then when he did finally pull away it would only hurt more because she would have fallen ever deeper in love with him during that time...

Yet Darcie didn't think anything could hurt as much as her heart did now. And now there was more than uncertainty, there was something more insidious, more dangerous. Now there was curiosity—and it brought along its even more dangerous cousin—the thinnest thread of *hope*. Because he'd shut down so quickly—hiding his emotions, his thinking. Because that's what he did when he was vulnerable. So did how he felt about her make him vulnerable in some way?

Don't dream. She tried to contain that unhelpful ache. In the morning she made herself a *plan*. Practical, achievable, realistic. She was a survivor and that's what survivors did. Firstly she needed a bigger flat if she were going to apply to foster Lily on her own. For that she needed work. But she had good skills and with a decent internet connection she should be able to get enough contract work she could complete from home until Lily was school age. Then she'd look for school hours. She signed up with her old agency and added another couple, finally in a place where she was no longer afraid to fully fight for this. She finally believed in herself enough to do this on her own.

The knock on her door startled her. For a second she froze, and then that hope—horrible, breath-stealing hope—skyrocketed. Hand pressed to her chest, she rose on tiptoe to check the security peephole. But while it was a familiar face, it was not the one she wanted. She opened the door and leaned against the edge as disappointment sucked the strength from her limbs.

'Hey, Shaun,' she muttered. 'You okay?'

He regarded her sombrely, guilt flickering as he nodded. 'Are you?'

She nodded and stepped back.

'I won't come in,' he said quickly. 'I just wanted to tell you I've reversed that payment. Your money should show in your account in a couple of hours.'

She blinked. That was so *not* what she'd expected. 'But what about your business? I really want you to have a crack at that…it's okay. Honestly.'

'It's not okay.' He sighed and looked skyward

for a second. 'I'm sorry, Darcie. And so ashamed. You know I struggle…to commit to anything much. Anyone. And I avoid the…chances.'

For a moment Darcie couldn't speak. Those words—those issues—struck deep within her. 'I know. I get it.'

Because she was the same. It was the legacy of having chances offered, then stolen away too many times. Of having dreams flattened and unfulfilled. After a while one avoided reaching for them. One avoided the *risk*.

'I don't need the marriage thing to try to get Lily,' she said, trying to reassure him. 'That was just me being insecure about my own abilities, too.' She offered a wan smile. 'But I want you to have the money. You can pay me back once you're up and running and can afford to, but don't give up this chance.' She wanted *one* of them to succeed in *something* and she knew he could make a go of this if he let himself really try.

'I'm not,' Shaun said gruffly. 'I found another backer.'

'You did?' The wind was sucked from her lungs again. 'Oh.'

He didn't need her.

'Actually, he found me.' Shaun looked rueful. 'Turns out that guy's actually okay. I was the jerk. I should have been in touch so much sooner. But I…' He shrugged.

Darcie stared, stuck on what—who—he meant. "That guy?' Was he talking about *Elias*? 'Are you saying Elias has given you the funding?'

'He, uh, wanted to keep it quiet but I didn't want to hide it from you, Darcie.' He dragged in a breath. 'It's great you want to help Lily and I really hope it works out… I'm sorry…'

'It's okay.' She realised how much it hurt to be reminded of someone you loved and had lost. 'I shouldn't have asked you. It was me being afraid to fight on my own.'

'Yeah.' He shifted on his feet awkwardly. 'I'd better go.'

Darcie nodded, needing the space to think. 'Thanks. Stay in touch, okay?'

'Okay.'

She closed the door and leaned against it. Elias had tracked Shaun down. He'd ensured she had her savings back. He'd offered to give Shaun a chance instead of trying to make him pay. When had he done all that? Why? Was he still trying to help her—still feeling sorry for her? Was it only because she'd refused to take his money that he'd made sure she got her own back?

The silence in the office was suffocating. The place was all but dead. His employees were all head down, hardworking, pushing to please him. It should have been great; instead, it sucked.

He missed seeing her there—*all* aspects of her. He missed efficient assistant Darcie, helping him in more ways than he'd let himself acknowledge. He missed hungry Darcie, surreptitiously snacking on cheese and nuts at the back of the boardroom, and he missed fiery Darcie. Demanding Darcie. Darcie who'd laughed—at him, with him. And breathless Darcie, he missed her, too.

And he didn't actually care enough anymore about any of the damn deals to be bothered working on them. Work just wasn't the same. Nothing was. It was supposedly the safe outlet for his demanding tendencies. The place where he could be in control, have the power. It was important and necessary and where he never lost emotional control. It was all paperwork—nothing personal. Only now he saw the ghost of Darcie everywhere. And he thought once again back to that crazy day in his office when she'd been late and he'd been unbelievably angry and then she'd declared she was leaving for her wedding.

He'd all but lost his mind. He'd not stopped to think. He'd just followed her and then there'd been no real reason for offering to step in as her groom other than that he couldn't stand to see her distressed. She'd been upset and angry and he'd just wanted to make everything better. He'd wanted to please her. But there had been a reason for that. A much bigger, much deeper reason that he'd refused to admit. He'd wanted her for *himself.* Because he cared about her. That was why he'd been so angry. He'd had her there in the one way that he could—as his assistant. She was his—working with him, spending all her time with him. But really he'd wanted so much more. Stripped back raw, he just wanted Darcie. And the Darcie that he'd got to know in the week since she'd walked out? He wanted that Darcie most of all.

Unfettered, unafraid Darcie was vibrant and playful. But there had been a time when she'd had to get drunk to summon the confidence to ask what she wanted from him. She'd been hurt; she'd lost almost everyone important in her life. She'd learned to *avoid* the things she wanted *most.*

He sat very still, realising then just what a colossal idiot he was.

He'd been upset at her reaction to that postnup—but her reaction was *everything.*

Because she'd stood up to him. She'd called him out. She'd expressed her desires. And he'd listened, he'd acted on them. He'd respected them—as she said he always did. Which meant he *wasn't* trying to control her and if he ever tried to? She'd soon let him know. She'd soon put him in his place. Darcie was stronger than anyone he knew and he was not like his father. Not in this.

But he *had* still failed her. Because he hadn't told her *his* desires. He'd not explained what *he* really wanted and why he wanted it. And most importantly how *he* truly felt. And she deserved—in fact *needed*—to know that. Darcie needed not just to be shown but told. Darcie needed more evidence than anyone before she could believe. So he needed to fight for her. For them. *Now*.

Darcie couldn't stop her mind from going in circles. She'd done the right thing, hadn't she? She couldn't stay in an arrangement in which her emotional needs weren't being met. She couldn't let Lily have that as her relationship role model. It was better for them both for Darcie to be independent.

She wanted more for Elias, too. She wanted him to feel the same emotional freedom and security she wanted for Lily. For him to know that he could speak up. That he *could* lose control and know he wasn't ever going to become a monster. And that he would still be loved. Always.

She knew how to love like that. She'd loved her best friend Zara, she loved Lily. She'd fallen in love with Elias. And she loved him so hard.

But she needed to be loved that way in return. That was what she was going to do for Lily. Lily would never again know what it was like to be unloved or unwanted or forgotten. She would never learn to be afraid of being honest—of being rejected for it. To be afraid of being out of control and wanting things. If she was lucky enough to succeed, she'd give Lily a home where it was safe to express her emotions. To say what she really felt and thought and not be judged for any of it. Not be rejected.

Darcie had *never* had that. So she'd kept her thoughts and her feelings to herself. But that wasn't to say she didn't have them. Of *course* she had them. And yes, she was sad and lonely now. But she'd recover. She still had Lily to focus on. She would rebuild her career, too. Her heart was broken but she would survive. That's what she always did. But being abandoned was the worst—feeling unwanted, knowing she was alone again—it sucked.

Her conscience pricked. Elias hadn't abandoned her. She'd all but asked him to leave. And she'd run away before he had the chance to because she'd thought it was inevitable what with that contract he'd wanted her to sign. But she'd not stopped to give him a chance to explain *why* it was so important to him. Instead she'd assumed the worst because she *always* assumed the worst.

But what if she was wrong? What if there was something more to it? He respected her boundaries. He always had—in fact he had a big thing about ensuring there was power balance between them. And given his parents' marriage she didn't blame him for being worried about the imbalance between them. He would never move to stop her if she'd made her wishes clear. And she had. Very quickly. Before he'd had a chance to say all that much.

But she hadn't made her *feelings* clear. She hadn't told him how she felt about him because she'd been scared and embarrassed. But maybe she needed to because she'd never felt like this before. And she wasn't sure he'd heard it before, either—from anyone. He meant so much to her surely she owed it to herself to speak up and give herself the chance?

Or at the very least to have the practice of opening up. And if he rejected her, it couldn't hurt worse than it already did, right? How could she not find the courage to do this when his actions subsequent to her leaving had given her the hope that perhaps he cared more than he'd let on? Perhaps he'd let her go precisely *because* he cared. Because he was trying to do what *she* wanted.

She had to give herself the chance to find out. She had to give *them* the chance. And she had to do it now.

CHAPTER SIXTEEN

IT WAS JUST before lunchtime when Darcie walked into the plush vestibule of Greyson VC.

'Darcie?' Olly, Elias's driver, was just inside the doors and looked stunned, then concerned, to see her. 'I thought—'

'Where is he?' she interrupted. She didn't want to know what Olly thought. She didn't want to lose her confidence now she finally had it. She needed to maintain her momentum before fear forced her give up and run away. Again. This was too important. 'Can you take me to him?' she asked, awkwardly breathless.

'Of course.' Olly was moving before she'd even finished asking.

Twenty minutes later, in the rear of the sleek, discreet sedan, Darcie's heart pounded as she recognised the streets she'd bussed through only an hour ago. She leaned forward so Olly could hear her. 'Are we...?'

'I dropped him at your flat almost an hour ago.' Olly nodded.

Darcie flopped back as her pulse sprinted. Elias had come to see her? Why? What had he wanted to say? Would he be waiting for her or would he have given up already? A billion thoughts crowded in, almost overwhelming her. 'Is he still there?'

'I don't know.' Olly shrugged apologetically. 'But he hasn't called me to collect him yet. He said he wouldn't need me for the rest of the day.'

Her pulse went supersonic then. What did he want? The yearning to know was so severe she began to shake and suddenly she was terrified he'd have left already. If he had then she'd have to gather the strength to find him again and right now she didn't know if her central nervous system could cope.

The second Olly pulled over she escaped the car and hurried towards the stairwell, convincing herself that of course he'd have gone already. It was ages since Olly had left him. She stared down at each step as she raced up the two flights and got herself breathless and most definitely prepared for the worst. So when she almost tripped over the man sitting on the top step she was shocked all over again.

'Oh!' She halted on the landing just past him and spun back to face him.

He'd remained seated, half leaning against the cold concrete wall. He wasn't in a suit but jeans and tee and while he'd shaved there were shadows in his face—beneath his eyes, his cheekbones—making his classically perfect features more prominent. It had only been a couple of days yet he'd developed a stark edge that made her poor heart ache even more.

'Darcie?' He rose to his feet in a swift movement, and just as he was about to step towards her he suddenly froze.

'What are you doing here?' She didn't recognise her own voice.

'Waiting for you.'

Yes, but why?

She bit her lip. She needed to say her own thing first. She needed to explain why she'd pushed away the other day. She needed to tell him—

'I had to see you,' he said, filling the gap. 'I'm sorry.'

The last thing she ever wanted was for him to apologise for wanting to see her.

He looked down and ran his hand through his hair. 'I know you wanted space but—'

'I've just been to the office,' she blurted.

His gaze shot back to her.

'I went to see you.'

Elias's blood seemed to be rushing everywhere except where he needed it. His muscles were ready to work but his brain was AWOL. He tried to slow down. She'd gone to see him at the office? Why had she done that? He gazed into her beautiful eyes and what he saw within them made the most fragile tendrils of hope unfurl.

'Olly drove me back.' Her eyes filled as her voice weakened. 'I'm glad you're still here.'

Darcie had tried to find *him*. Something fierce and powerful flooded his system. *Right thing.* This was the right thing to have done. Seeing her—being near her—was so very right. But before he could touch her—and he wanted that more than his next breath—he had to tell her *why*. To explain, not assume. To be brave enough to be vulnerable.

'I wasn't leaving till I'd seen you.' He'd been willing to wait for as long as it took.

Her glance skittered away from him, then back. 'It's damp and hard in the stairwell.'

It was, but he didn't give a damn. The real problem was now that all the words, all the things he'd thought he'd say, had evaporated in this searing emotion of seeing her again. Of knowing she'd sought him out. There was only one thing he wanted, one thing he could say.

'Darcie,' he breathed. 'Come home.'

She just stared at him—frozen—but at least not fleeing. He watched her remain locked so tightly wound, so very still. And then twin tears spilled from her eyes. It wrecked him completely.

'Please.' He stepped towards her; he couldn't not. 'I miss you. It's our home. You're my wife, Darcie. For real. And I love you.'

Her lips parted but still she didn't say anything.

'Darcie...' He huffed out a breath. 'I didn't know how to deal with everything I was feeling and I screwed up.'

'What did you say?'

'That I didn't know—'

'Before that.'

He paused and felt that kick in his heart. 'That I love you.'

She blinked rapidly. Swallowed. He knew she was battling to hold it together. He didn't want her to hold anything together and certainly hold nothing back. Not now. He'd put it on the line and ached to know everything she was thinking and feeling and wanting. But he also knew she wasn't quite able to yet.

'It's a first for me,' he said quietly. 'And I really don't know what I'm doing. I thought I could manage it but...' He shook his head. 'I got so tangled up in stressing about having too much power, that you were only with me because you'd had no real choice. That you needed work. That it was gratitude. That it was just lust. That you'd never really feel the same as what I do because there's *always* been another layer or ten in our relationship. And I've been so scared of turning into my father. You know when you're told something over and over you begin to believe it. Especially when you're told by someone important in your life.'

Darcie nodded. She understood. She'd been told she wasn't welcome, wasn't wanted, wasn't worthy—but not as often as his father had talked all that rubbish to him, yet it had been enough to sink in and stay lodged deep beneath the surface. Those lies were hard to dig out and let go of.

'But I'm not like him,' Elias said. 'In fact, in this, I've been more like my mother—not speaking up, *not* saying what needed to be said. Not saying how I really felt. I promised myself that I'd always do whatever you asked me to. That I wouldn't stop you from doing things you wanted. That I wouldn't ever try to control you. So the other day when you insisted on leaving, I couldn't stop you. But I should have told you things before you left. I should have explained *why* I really wanted you to sign that thing. Why I didn't want you to go. I wasn't honest with you, Darcie.'

He drew breath. 'To be honest I was too upset to even think. Like that day back at the office when you reminded me you resigned and then told me you were getting married. I just re-acted. I was so angry. I've never been as angry and I sure didn't stop to consider why I was so blinded with emotion that I crashed into chairs on the way out. Why was I literally running to stop you? Why was I willing to do anything when I realised how badly I'd upset you? To try to fix things.' He shook his head. 'It's so bloody obvious, Darcie, but we've both been too blin-kered—too scared—to see the whole picture. You weren't going to be in my life anymore and that wasn't just intolerable, that unlocked something in me that couldn't be forced back into the box it had been in forever. My heart, Darcie. You unlocked my heart. And not just the capacity to love but to feel everything—fear, jealousy, anger, resentment...*all* the things. And frankly on paper all those scary things outnum-ber love. They really do. They were all things I *never* wanted to feel. But then I realised love weighs more. It's *worth* more. And having you in my life is worth everything.'

She nodded—half crying, half laughing, un-bearably relieved. Elias would never normally pour out his heart and she could see it was a strain for him to do it now. She could see the sheen on his skin, the uncharacteristic stum-bling over words when he normally was effi-ciently eloquent.

'I used to think being left was the worst. Being alone. But it's not.' Her eyes burned and as she blinked more tears fell. 'It's having some-one put up with you because they feel they *have* to, not because they *want* to. I couldn't stand it if I became a burden to you, Elias. I was so worried that would happen and then that you'd only resent me while I'd come to hate you because I want *so* much more than the passionless marriage we originally agreed to.'

'You want more?'

'I want *everything*,' she breathed. 'I want everything to be real. I want you and I want Lily and I want more children, too. With you.' And now Darcie's heart swelled to bursting because he wanted her to come *home*. 'You were worried about always having some kind of power over me, right?'

He nodded.

'You wanted me to be free—not to feel any obligation. That's why you brought that horrible contract home.'

He nodded again. 'I didn't realise you'd think it was horrible. I wanted you to be free to choose whatever you wanted. I wanted to give you everything.'

He'd tried to do it all—without her having to ask.

'So here's the thing,' she said huskily. 'I guess I've got pretty good at avoiding being hurt. But I've also got good at avoiding having to trust anyone. It's easier *not* to believe that someone will be there for me. Sometimes homes didn't want me but other times, I *chose* to escape before they could reject me.' She swallowed hard. 'Your rejection would destroy me,' she admitted. 'So when I saw that contract, I ran before you could do that. Because I didn't think you'd ever want me the way I wanted you to want me—'

'But you're wrong.'

'Maybe.' She caught the look in his eye and bit her lip. 'Okay, wrong,' she whispered. 'But I was so scared, Elias. And I'm sorry for that. But I realised I needed to be brave and tell you how I feel.' She rose on tiptoe and whispered to him. 'That's why I came to find you.'

She saw the flicker in his eyes. The shadow of vulnerability that she'd felt so deeply herself for so long. Her handsome, strong lover wasn't as invincible as he'd like his business opponents to believe. He was as human as she. As capable of being as hurt. And so, reaching for a kind of courage she'd never required more than now, she looked him straight in the eyes and told him the truth. 'I choose *you*, Elias,' she breathed, ignoring the tears still slowly tracking down her cheeks. This was too important to hold back or to be embarrassed about just how much emotion she was showing. 'I choose to be with you and I really hope you choose me back.'

'You know I already have,' he muttered

roughly. 'But seeing you this upset is killing me, Darcie—'

'Then hold me together,' she begged. 'Just hold me.'

He shook his head but walked towards her at the same time. 'If I do that I'll never let you go.'

'Good.'

She saw the most gorgeous smile light up his face but then he was there, pulling her close and she closed her eyes in pure relief. His arms wrapped tightly around her and she heard his husky broken whisper into her hair.

'Don't ask me to let you go again, Darcie. I don't think I could stand it.'

'I don't want you to. Not ever. I love you.'

His arms tightened even more and it was heavenly. She lifted her chin and he met her lips. She was instantly transported, instantly warmed—from heartbreak to heaven in his kiss, his hold, his love.

'We, uh, need to get into your flat,' he muttered breathlessly.

'We do,' she gasped.

It took too long to fumble with the key but as soon as they were inside she was back in his arms. They stumbled together working through the swift, desperate dispatch of clothing and the feverish seeking of touch. Of connection. Of love. And when he finally, fiercely thrust home she cried out with utter joy. They moved together—fast and frantic, feverish and urgent—as if neither believed this was actually real and they were together again. Only then they were—moving as one, locked in sync with each other, driven to the sublime moment where the stars burst and bodies simply shook.

'Darcie!'

Absolute completion followed. And then, when heartbeats slowed and breath was caught, words returned.

'Feeling nothing—or nothing too deeply—was easy,' he murmured warmly. 'But it wasn't honest. Because I still felt everything. I just pretended I didn't. I just buried my emotions and made myself busy with other things. But they were still there until with you I couldn't bury it any more. Life is too good with you in it,' he groaned. 'We're *made* for each other.'

'We belong together.'

He cupped her face. 'I'm so sorry you've been denied this for so long. But no more being alone, okay? You have me now. Always.'

She'd never belonged to anyone before. Not like this. And he knew. Now she understood his intention the other day. She'd been too scared to believe it could be anything other than rejection when in fact it was the complete opposite and if she'd had just a little more confidence, a little more faith, she'd have known that then.

'I saw Shaun today.'

Elias looked at her astutely.

'You might lose your money.'

'That's less of a problem for me than it is for you.' Elias said gently. 'You worked so hard for your independence.'

'So did you.'

'And I'm a lot further along that path than you are.' He rolled his shoulders and shot her a half smile. 'I invest in all kinds of enterprises.'

'Not usually small owner-operated courier businesses.'

'He's an okay guy.' Elias sighed. 'He feels terrible.'

'I know,' she said softly. 'But you didn't want me to know.' She drew in a little breath. 'You didn't want me to be grateful for that, either?' She shook her head when he didn't answer. 'You don't want me to be grateful for anything? It's not going to work like that, Elias. I am always, *always* going to be grateful for *you*.'

He bowed his head and rested his forehead against hers. 'I finally realised we're even,' he murmured. 'You have power over me. Total power.' He cupped her hands in his. 'Because you hold my heart. I'm hoping you won't crush it and throw it away.'

'Never,' she promised, crowding closer still. 'You don't have to change for me, Elias. Not in anyway. I just need *you* with me.'

She'd strived for everything alone for so long and to have him—the one she wanted more than anything at her side—helping her and loving her and promising never to leave her…was utterly overwhelming. It wasn't that she didn't believe him but that she couldn't believe it was real at all. 'Just promise me I'm not dreaming?'

His gaze turned tender. 'I'm here. And I promise I'm not going anywhere.' He pulled her to him. 'I breathe deeper with you. Feel more. Do more. You're the energy in my life and I'm not going to lose you. We'll do it all, have it all, together.' He smiled at her with all the love in the world. 'I've got you, Darcie Milne. And I'll hold you. Always.'

CHAPTER SEVENTEEN

Two years later

'COME BACK UPSTAIRS *to me...*'

Darcie's husky plea echoed in his head. She was still up in their bed and the last time he'd peeked he'd seen she'd fallen back to sleep. But he'd never ignore her request. He'd once said no to her. He'd never know how he actually did. And he never would again. Not when she'd been so wary of asking him for anything more. She'd been so afraid of rejection and abandonment, so untrusting, he was determined never to let her down again. He would be by her side any time and every time she asked. He'd slowed down on the mergers and acquisitions. He'd even sold off a couple of things. There wasn't the drive to accumulate as much anymore because he had other things to do. Like make breakfast in bed with his favourite little sidekick.

'She likes maple syrup,' Lily announced confidently.

'She does. Let's make sure we have plenty in the jug.' He winked at the little girl.

Lily had been with them for just over a year now—a permanent placement with adoption on the near horizon. And it was wonderful. Also wonderful were the more frequent lunch dates he had with his mother. Darcie came sometimes, too. And his mother had met Lily. It was one way in which he could enrich his mother's life— to just be there for her. Anytime she asked. And happily, she was asking more and more.

'She's having a really big sleep-in.' Lily said.

'Yeah.' Darcie had been tired lately and Elias had his suspicions as to why, but he was waiting for her to explain it to him.

'Will she be okay?'

'Of course.' Elias smiled reassuringly at Lily. 'Especially once she's had our amazing breakfast.'

When he opened the bedroom door for Lily, Darcie was sitting up in bed. Her smile widened as she watched Lily carefully carry the laden breakfast tray. 'That looks amazing, Lily. I love pancakes.'

But Elias noticed—with an inward smile— that it was the piece of plain toast Darcie picked up first.

'I've got swimming today,' Lily chirruped as she tore a piece of pancake from the plate. 'And then reader's club.'

'Yes.' Darcie smiled. 'Are you enjoying the book?'

Lily nodded. 'Elias and I finished it just before making you breakfast.'

'Time to go, Lily,' Elias said. 'Nanny's downstairs waiting to walk you to school.'

'You're not walking me today?'

Walking Lily to the school down the road was one of Elias's favourite ways to start the day. 'I can't this morning, sweetie.'

'Because you're looking after Darcie?'

'Yes,' he said seriously.

'Feel better soon.' Lily blew Darcie a kiss and then skipped out of the room calling for her nanny.

Elias turned back to Darcie and saw the emotion misting her eyes. 'Did you sleep okay?'

'I slept really well.' She bit her lip. 'But the silly thing is, I'm still really tired.'

He lifted the tray from her lap and put it on the table before returning to sit on the edge of the bed. 'Is that so very silly?'

'Maybe not,' she murmured. 'You know I have a secret...' She swallowed.

'Yeah... Good secret?' He asked huskily.

She nodded and a tear fell from her eye. 'The best.'

His heart swelled.

'But I think you've guessed already.' She gestured towards the breakfast tray she'd barely touched. 'Plain toast. Orange juice. Bottle of multivitamins?' Her giggle was watery and divine.

'But am I right?' Now his heart was about to burst. 'I really hope I'm right, Darcie.'

'Lily's going to be a big sister,' she whispered. 'We're going to have a baby.'

'Oh, Darcie.' He wrapped his arms around her and held her tightly. She was the centre of his world.

'Thank you.' Darcie pressed her face into his chest, her tears spilling. 'Thank you, thank you.'

'Darcie?' He framed her face in his hands.

She gazed up at him. 'You've given me everything. *Everything.*'

'Ditto.'

Darcie melted into the kiss and felt that familiar hunger kick. She would never, ever get enough of her handsome husband.

'I did the test this morning, while you were downstairs with Lily.' She'd been so nervous, so excited. 'So you're not going in to the office today?' She smiled.

'How can I?' he asked with mock innocence. 'You told me to come back to bed.'

She giggled.

'So I figure you're not going in to the office either,' he winked.

She wasn't. She'd taken on a job working for an organisation upskilling vulnerable women so they could take charge of their personal finances, re-enter the workforce if they'd been out a while, or escape unsafe situations. It was rewarding and invigorating. But while she loved it, she needed the break today to celebrate this moment with him.

'What are we going to do instead?' She felt that greediness open up inside her. Having Elias all to herself was such a treat.

'We're taking some leisure time. We're going to lunch at your favourite restaurant and later, when Lily gets home, we're taking the jet somewhere warm and sunny for our babymoon.'

Her jaw dropped. 'Babymoon?'

He looked smug. 'A little break before the baby arrives. I have plans for us to take a few, actually.'

'A few?' She giggled. 'You really did guess my secret.'

'Uh-huh.' He leaned closer. 'Are you okay with the idea?'

She nodded. She was very okay with it.

'But first I'm going to pamper you *personally*.'

'Oh?' she murmured. 'That sounds good.'

His wolfish smile flashed. 'I thought so.'

Making love to her husband was the most luscious thing in the world. How had she ever thought he was controlled and unemotional? When he breathed his vows to her she wrapped herself around him like a limpet. He choked, a little laugh, a cry of such relief in the ecstasy they shared, and the bliss that then flooded through her was enhanced all the more.

And later, when she was sleepy all over again, she laced her fingers through his and marvelled at all they'd built together.

'Lily has her place in the world. She's surrounded by people who love her,' she mumbled dreamily. Together they were like a net—holding her in security and love and with strength in their unity. It was everything she'd ever wanted for the girl. And for herself. She rolled to face him as her emotions wobbled out of control again. 'And so am I.'

'Yes.' He brushed back her hair and his smile was lopsided. 'We love you. So very much.'

She knew. She believed him. And she loved him right back.

'I didn't think I would ever be this lucky,' she breathed.

'I know. But it's not luck,' he said. 'You deserve it, Darcie. We all do.' His lips curved. 'Even me.'

She smiled tremulously, accepting it all and adoring the fact that he did, too.

Love had won.

* * * * *